CW00487155

LAST RIDE

LAST RIDE

DENISE YOUNG

HARPER **PERENNIAL**

Harper Perennial
An imprint of HarperCollins*Publishers*

First published in 2004
This edition published in 2009
by HarperCollins*Publishers* Australia Pty Limited
ABN 36 009 913 517
www.harpercollins.com.au

HarperCollins*Publishers*
25 Ryde Road, Pymble, Sydney, NSW 2073, Australia
31 View Road, Glenfield, Auckland 0627, New Zealand
1–A, Hamilton House, Connaught Place, New Delhi – 110 001, India
77–85 Fulham Palace Road, London, W6 8JB, United Kingdom
2 Bloor Street East, 20th floor, Toronto, Ontario M4W 1A8, Canada
10 East 53rd Street, New York NY 10022, USA

National Library of Australia Cataloguing-in-Publication data:

Young, Denise.
   Last ride.
   ISBN 978 0 7322 8997 3 (pbk.)
   I. Title.
A823.4

Cover photograph by Rhys Graham
Author photograph courtesy Andy Doldissen
Cover design by Darren Holt, HarperCollins Design Studio
Typeset in Bembo 11.5/16pt by HarperCollins Design Studio
Printed and bound in Australia by Griffin Press
50gsm Bulky News used by HarperCollins*Publishers* is a natural, recyclable
product made from wood grown in sustainable plantation forests. The
manufacturing processes conform to the environmental regulations in the
country of origin, New Zealand.

5 4 3 2 1   09 10 11 12 13

In memory of my dear friend,
Jonathan Dennis.

CONTENTS

CHAPTER ONE

ESCAPE

Kev is throwing clothes and tins of food into his black bag. Chook hangs watching, torn between his dad's urgency and the broken body of Max. He shivers, still damp from the cold water he's used to get the blood off. No chance to light the chip heater. He wraps his arms round his bare chest. He's got no idea what the time is, only that it's late. He was in a deep sleep when the noises woke him.

'Hurry up! Grab your stuff!' Kev says.

Chook picks up a flannelette shirt and drops it into his bag.

'Oh, great! One shirt! Get a fuckin move on or I'll go without you!' Kev shoves Chook's bag towards him.

'What about Max? Shouldn't we . . .'

'Leave him. You seen me check on him. He'll be all right.'

1

Chook looks at the bed. Max seems very still and grey under the spatters of blood, his wayward hair spread across the stained pillow. His chest isn't moving, at least not as far as Chook can see. He turns away to hide the tears starting in his eyes. While he is bending down to pull on his tracksuit pants, he half sees his dad going through the pockets of Max's trousers where they hang over the chair and taking out his car keys and wallet.

Chook puts on his shoes and finds a T-shirt in the mess of clothing on the floor. He picks the rest of it up and dumps it into his bag, then pulls on his cap. His dad is already halfway out the bedroom door, grabbing his jacket as he goes.

'Dad . . .'

Kev pauses.

'Can't we get him a doctor?'

'I told you. He'll live. He's knocked out, that's all.'

Kev goes out the door. Chook is about to follow him but stops. He has to take his cars. They're lumped under his pillow and scattered all over the floor. He can hear the engine of Max's ute starting up. Quick. He panics and stuffs as many as he can into each of his pockets, hoping he's got the Mazda RX7 and the white Mustang convertible with the blue stripe, and races out without looking again over towards the bed.

'Shut the door,' Kev shouts over the revving. Chook

2

slams the front door and flings his bag with his dad's in the back of the ute. In the distance he can hear Max's dog, Holy Terror, Terror for short, barking, as if he knows something's happening. Max always chains him up for the night outside his place. Chook jumps into the passenger seat of the ute. His dad squeals the tyres as they take off into the night, bumping over the cattle grid that leads off the property and hitting the dirt road east. When he looks back, Chook can see their bags sliding around and banging against the sides of the tray. They should have tied them down but there's no way his dad will stop now.

Chook checks the cars he's collected. Yes, the Mustang is there with the RX7, his lucky car, as well as the red Porsche and the Swiss army knife he keeps in that pocket, just in case. In the other pocket he's got the Corvette, the Valiant Charger, the Camaro and the good old Hummer. He thinks about the others left behind and crosses his fingers that they'll be able to get back for them, as well as for Striker, the mountain bike with special handles, and the gold sovereigns Max gave him. Max. He puts Max's bloody face and the way his eyes rolled back in his head out of his mind. He presses his knuckles into his eye sockets hard and pulls his cap down low over his eyes.

Kev looks at him. 'You OK?'

'Yes,' he lies. 'Where are we going?'

'I'm not sure yet. Let's see where the road takes us.'

The road will take them to Sofala, Chook knows that. They bounce over the rocky track at speed, as they have hundreds of times. The trees on either side of the road look like startled ghosts trapped in the light, the road forever coming towards them and sliding away. The darkness hides the stony hills around as the ute pounds down towards the valley.

Suddenly his dad swerves violently to avoid hitting a roo pinned in the headlights. He swears as the car nearly loses it. Chook realises it's exactly the same spot where they went over the edge in their own car and totalled it. His dad was stoned that night and driving the car in angel gear, the gear stick in neutral, Kev yahooing, Chook yelling 'stop' and grabbing onto anything he could find, as they careered down the hill out of control. They rolled twice before a tree saved them. Kev and Chook walked away without a scratch, but the car was a write-off.

That was the second time it happened. The other time was worse. They rolled his dad's mate Huey's car up at Taylor's Arm last year. He and his dad walked away from that as well but Huey wasn't so lucky. That's another thing Chook's trying to forget. He knows cats have nine lives, but people usually only get one. He and his dad have had two so far. There won't be a third.

He clutches at the door and hunkers down further in his seat. They shouldn't be doing this, he knows, leaving Max. He can feel the familiar knot in his stomach he always gets when his dad completely loses it with someone and goes right off. His body keeps on shaking, though it isn't cold. He wishes there'd been time to get the money he's got saved for an emergency in the tin buried out the back. This feels like an emergency.

His dad is concentrating on driving. He smells of beer and stale tobacco. Chook sees him hunching forward in his seat, battling the road. The night escape and the way his dad smells reminds Chook of leaving the Valley nearly a year ago, only that was fun. He and his dad and Dianne jigged round in their seats and partied hard all the way south.

They meet the tar with a jolt outside Sofala and then take the Bathurst road, powering uphill, the few tumbledown houses silent and dark, their owners tucked up safe in bed. Chook's eyes are getting droopy in spite of himself. So we're going to Bathurst, he thinks drowsily. Maybe his dad will find a doctor there for Max.

He's falling. It's dark. He knows there are high cliffs round him, monster cliffs that look like the ones his dad jumped off once with him on his back. They

5

landed in a deep rock pool with a stinging splash that time. He lost his dad for a moment in the water and tasted the salt in his mouth. Salt tastes like panic when you can't swim.

He doesn't know if he jumped or fell or was pushed this time. He's scared and tries to call out 'Dad!' but the word won't come out.

He goes on falling through the dark forever. He's counting the seconds and minutes under his breath when he stops suddenly. There's no bump. It doesn't even hurt. He realises the cliffs have moved in to save him. They're hugging him, so tight that he can't move. Pressing and pressing, hard against him. He's glad at first, but then they keep moving in, tight, tighter, so he's being squashed. He tries again to shout out to his dad but he's got no breath.

When they first rocked up to Max's farm after the drive from Taylor's Arm, it was just starting to get light. Chook realised he'd fallen asleep on the back seat. Max's face peering in at the car window was a blur of grey whiskers and pink light making a halo round his wisps of hair. He saw his dad getting out of the car and holding his hand out and Max shaking it. He saw them start talking, his dad bending to Max's stoop.

'Your dad reckons Max owes him,' Dianne whispered to Chook, looking round from the front seat, her red hair springing up wild from her head and her eyes sleepy.

'He does,' Chook whispered back. 'He and my dad owned a dog together once before I was born and my dad never got paid what he should of, from the winnings. My dad always said he was going to come back one day and get his money.'

Chook loved watching the dogs and he was good at picking winners. He used to take a long look at the field, then point one dog out, say 'that one' and his dad would put money on it. It came in nine times out of ten. Almost.

Kev leaned back in to the car and jerked his head for them to get out.

'We'll be staying here for a bit. Max reckons he can do with a hand.'

'What about your money, Dad?' Chook asked urgently, as Max led the way into his house, scratching his bottom through pants that hung off his bony hips.

'Mind your own business,' his dad said.

Max was standing by the front door, holding it open. They walked in and hovered in an uneasy knot just inside, while Max went away to put on the kettle.

'Are we staying in this house?' Chook asked his dad.

'No, down the road a coupla ks. There's an empty place he said we can have.'

'What am I going to do with myself here?' Dianne asked.

'What I tell you,' Kev said and put his hand on her bottom. Chook saw her lean against him for a moment and rest her head on his chest.

Chook was swaying with tiredness as well. Why couldn't they go straight to the empty house? Why did they always have to have cups of tea?

Max came out with a tray. On it there were four tin mugs, milk, sugar and a teapot, as well as a big plate of biscuits. Chook woke up a bit when he saw the biscuits.

'Go on,' Max said to him. 'Eat up.'

Chook took one biscuit, with a glance at his dad for approval.

'Gawd,' Max said, 'one's not going to fill you up. Take a handful.'

Chook took a handful, as they all perched on rickety chairs round an old wooden table with deep scratch marks on the top. Chook thought it looked as if some animal had gone wild in there.

'Yairs,' Max said, pouring tea for all of them and adding sugar and milk without asking. 'I could do with your help. It's too much for me on my own.'

Dianne yawned suddenly as she took her tea, showing a mouth alive with sharp white teeth.

'Pardon,' she said, covering her mouth too late.

'Keeping you up, are we?' Max asked, stirring vigorously.

'Long drive,' she said.

'You can have a snooze soon enough. The place hasn't been lived in for a while, but. You might be sharing it with a bit of wildlife.'

'Oh, great,' said Dianne, looking at Kev.

'We can handle the wildlife, no worries,' Kev said.

Depends, Chook thought, slurping his sweet tea. Possums could go pretty stir crazy if they were trapped inside. Up in the shack they borrowed from Huey near Taylor's Arm, a possum ripped their only curtain to bits once trying to get away from his dad, when he was in a rage with it for stealing their food. Even possums knew better than to hang round when his dad went ballistic. That one finally shot up the chimney in a shower of soot. His dad lit a fire but it got away. The trouble was, the shack had a big hole in the roof so it was easy for possums to get in, but when it came to getting out again they couldn't find the way. Whenever it rained it was like a waterfall and he and his dad slept in the Falcon parked outside.

Max was handing a key on a piece of string to Kev.

Kev wiped tea from his beard before he took the key and stood up. Dianne and Chook stood too, Chook's legs nearly giving way on him. Dianne grabbed him and helped him out to the car, both of them staggering like drunks heading home.

'I'll come round in the arvo,' Max promised, hitching his pants up. 'Give yer a chance to get some sleep.'

Chook heard Dianne say as they drove away: 'This better not be for long, Kev.'

But he didn't hear his dad answer.

Kev is shaking him awake.

'Hey,' Chook protests.

He opens his eyes and looks out the window. It's early morning, the sun just teasing the dark trees at the side of the road. They must have been driving all night.

'Are we here?' he asks.

'Where?' Kev answers, yawning.

'Where we're going,' Chook answers.

'We're nearly at Dubbo.'

'Oh,' says Chook. One place is much the same as another to him. In his almost eleven years he's lived in four states, Queensland, Tasmania, South Australia and New South Wales, never staying much more than twelve months in one place. His dad is all he's got, since his mum cleared out when he was two years old. She told his dad she was going shopping one day and never came back. Much later they heard from her friend, Mandy, that she was killed in a car accident, 'Good riddance,' his dad said. She was a bitch. She never even changed his nappy, or did anything for him when he was a baby. Chook doesn't want to think about those saggy brown nappies his dad said he would find him wearing when he came home from work. His mum just stayed in bed all day.

'Are we stopping at Dubbo?' he asks.

'Not for long. We'll leave the ute there.'

Max's ute. Memories come clawing back to Chook about what happened in the night. He hoped it was a nightmare. He remembers the smell of blood, of fear and violence, of his own terror. He can hear the sound of the thuds that woke him, his father's fists hollow against Max's skull, Max groaning, his blood getting on Chook as he tried to roll away.

He feels hot waves coming up from his stomach. He's going to be sick. His dad must see him trying to hold it in, because he grabs the cap off Chook's head and holds that to his chin while he swerves off the road and stops. The curdled, sharp smell of vomit fills the cabin of the ute.

'Fuckin hell,' Kev growls. 'Get out!'

Chook gets out with the cap full of vomit and bends over, waiting for the next wave to hit him. The fresh air seems to help. Nothing more comes up. He straightens and tips up the cap to empty it, scraping the sick mess on the grass by the side of the road. He turns to get back in the car.

'Leave that bloody thing,' Kev says. 'It stinks.'

'No,' says Chook. It's his favourite cap because his girlfriend Amber wrote her name on it. He's kept it for almost a year, ever since he left the little bush school where he met her. It was up near Taylor's Arm and only had twenty-five kids in it, if they all turned up. Six of them were Amber's cousins and one was her brother, they were all Morans, and her mum drove the school bus, so it felt like one big family.

The best part about it was that the kids were allowed to climb the trees in the playground. Everybody had their own tree, all sitting up in the branches at lunchtime, dotted round like gumnuts. There was a tree right near their classroom that rustled and whispered all day long. Tait Moran said it told your secrets and dobbed on you if you swore, but he and his brother Evan swore all day long and Mr Pike, the teacher, never heard, so it must not have been true.

The school had a vegetable garden and a pet rabbit called Twitch. Everybody got a turn taking Twitch home in the holidays, but Chook had to leave just when his turn was coming up. Again. His dad had an argument with a man in the Bowraville pub who broke his dad's rules: get out of my face once, get out of my face twice and then bam! He let you have it. Well, it was two rules and an action, really. The man didn't move after his dad hit him and they got out of there fast. Like now.

His dad told him and Dianne on the drive south what the fight was about. The man blamed his dad for Huey dying in the crash. The gun was on the back seat when they rolled the car. Chook didn't know how it went off but Huey copped it. His dad had nothing to do with it. It was an accident. He gets into a lot of blues like that with people over things that aren't his fault. His dad always says if you give a dog a bad name you might as well shoot it on the spot because it's done for.

Before his dad can stop him, he throws the cap in the back of the ute and gets in, slamming the door. His dad doesn't say any more about it. Chook decides he'll wash it when he gets a chance.

As they come into the town along the wide highway, the sky seems to brighten by the minute. They pass a KFC and pull up opposite McDonald's. It's got a big number six lit up outside, giving its opening time. Kev says they're right on the dot. He gets out and searches in his bag for scissors and a razor. The bag is a travelling survival kit. Apart from clothes, food and a billy can, he's got a torch, tools, sewing gear, string, tape, rope and bottles of coloured medicine. The two of them have never come within cooee of a doctor.

He gets back in and begins to cut his hair as Chook watches. It hangs down to his shoulders in greasy lengths, streaked here and there with grey. Often he drags it back into a ponytail. Now he cuts it above the ears at the sides and gets Chook to help where he can't see at the back. Chook's never cut anyone's hair before, so he takes off big clumps, while his dad keeps swearing at him for pulling too hard. It's good that Kev can't see the back, because it looks like Chook's hacked it with his Swiss army knife. When Chook hands him back the scissors, Kev shakes them at him as if he's about to take revenge.

'Your turn, boyo,' he says, through clenched teeth.

Chook tries to resist but you don't say no to his dad for long, not if you want to keep your teeth. Kev attacks the dirty blond tangle with determination. When he finishes, Chook looks in the rear vision mirror and pulls a face. He looks like one of Max's newly shorn merinos, complete with a little nick above his ear. He touches where it hurts and winces.

His dad says: 'No grizzling. You didn't hear me whingeing, did ya?'

Chook doesn't grizzle. He runs his fingers over his scalp, feeling how sharp and stubbly it is. When his dad gets out and carefully puts the scissors back in his bag, the wind is cold on Chook's head. Kev gets back into the car, putting his scratchy razor into his pocket in case there's hot water in the toilets for a shave, and drives into the car park alongside the low brick building.

CHAPTER TWO

DUBBO

They go in and order from a sleepy girl. Chook sees his dad pull out Max's wallet to pay. He knows that's wrong; it's stealing from your mate. Kev gets hash browns, a large Coke and an endless cup of coffee, while Chook has a Sausage and Egg McMuffin. He's glad to see the toy is a dinosaur head. Tyrannosaurus Rex, by the look of it. The girl smiles at him and slips it across the counter when the manager isn't looking, because you're only supposed to get toys with Happy Meals.

They take a seat at a table near the side window and look out at the deserted children's playground. It's made of plastic, coloured red, yellow and blue, with too much kiddy stuff for Chook. A tiny slide you could crawl down, hard balls to spin and cartoon characters chopped into three so you can mix and match. Chook grew out of all that years ago. He plays with the dinosaur head, leaving his food sitting there. It doesn't want to go down. His stomach is still tight as a drum.

Suddenly Kev stiffens. A police car has pulled into the car park. He nudges Chook and points it out.

'Don't look. Keep eating.'

Two cops get out of the car and come in slowly, looking round the way cops do. One is boulder shaped, while the other looks more like a long gloomy coat on a hanger with square shoulders and an axe face. Kev and Chook are the only customers and the cops give them a lingering stare. Chook pretends to eat the sausage while Kev chomps steadily on the hash browns.

The Boulder seems to know the girl at the counter. He calls her Lindy when he gives the order, while Axeface keeps staring at Kev and Chook. Chook wonders what it is about them that makes cops they've never seen before stare like they do. Is it his dad's tatts? Axeface whispers to the Boulder and they both nod. Axeface goes back out to the police car, giving Max's ute the once-over as he passes and taking note of the rego number. AFQ 638. Chook knows it off by heart, as well as the rego numbers of Max's farm bikes and every car they've ever had, which is quite a few. His dad reckons Chook's got a photographic memory for numbers.

Kev mutters to Chook: 'They'll run a rego check. Don't worry. It'll be cool.'

The Boulder is still chatting up the girl. They can see Axeface sitting in the police car fiddling with something. Chook sees sweat breaking out on his dad's neck as he puts three lots of sugar into his coffee and stirs. Chook nibbles on a piece of McMuffin, then rests his chin on his hands, studying the Mustang he's pulled out of his pocket. It's a really cool unit.

He sees out of the corner of his eye that Axeface has got out of the police car and is coming back inside. Neither Kev nor Chook looks towards him as he joins his mate and shakes his head. The cops collect their takeaways and leave. As they get into their car, his dad starts to relax. He reaches out and touches Chook's newly shorn hair.

'We passed, eh!'

'Passed what?' asks Chook.

'The rego check. Dumb fucks. Max is clean.'

Watching the police car pull out, Chook asks: 'How did they find out about us?'

'They didn't,' Kev says.

'What were they doing here then?'

'Having breakfast, same as us,' Kev snaps.

Chook shifts in his seat and doesn't say any more. His dad can flick the switch to menace in two shakes of a lamb's tail. Kev finishes his cup of coffee and goes to shave. It's even more important now the cops have clocked him, he tells Chook.

Left alone, Chook stops pretending to eat. He pulls out the Porsche and the RX7 and gives them a bit of a spin across the table. His small cars irritate the hell out of Kev, so he plays with them when Kev isn't there. It was OK around Max; in fact, Max gave him most of the best cars he's got. The two of them would sit up and watch car racing on television when Max babysat him. Not that he needed babysitting. He is no baby. He shivers and shakes his head to clear Max out. Just thinking about him makes his stomach go tight again. He concentrates hard on his cars.

He's driving the RX7 and leading in the Grand Prix when it spins out of control, runs off the track and Michael Schumacher, in the Porsche, flies past him. Damn. Just his luck. He's getting his car back up and ready for the next race when his dad comes out, looking fresh and scrubbed. Chook jams his cars into his pocket as Kev sits down. He runs his hands over his dad's cheeks to feel the smoothness.

'You missed this bit,' he points out.

'It'll have to do,' Kev says. 'That razor's past its use by.'

Suddenly Chook remembers his hat. He gets up and goes out to the ute. When he comes back with it, his dad tells him to dump it, but Chook goes into the men's toilet without answering.

The smell of it is horrible. He wets it under the tap and watches as the water turns yellowish and bits of vomit fall off into the basin and go down the drain. He rinses it for a long while. When he finishes, he has a sniff of it. It still smells a bit sick, but he thinks it'll wear off. He comes out with the soaking hat in his hands. His father isn't there. He looks out into the car park. The ute is gone.

Panic sweeps through him. He runs towards the counter, then madly back out to the car park, turning round and round like a weathervane in a willy-willy. 'Dad!' he calls to the empty world. He is nowhere. In front of him there's another fast food place, where a stiff red rooster hangs silent against the blue sky. The bottle shop next door has a sign outside, with two wobbly shapes on it that look like noses. It's closed. The whole place is deserted. Chook looks back once more towards Macca's. The girl is watching him with a worried look on her face. He turns back and sits down on the entry ramp, the wet hat dripping between his knees and a cold southerly wind tugging at his T-shirt and sending icy chills through his bristly hair.

A car horn sounds. Max's ute squeals to a stop at the end of the ramp and his father's grinning face looks up at him, his arm hanging casually out the window. Chook is furious. He stomps round the back of the ute clutching the cap, gets in the passenger side and sits down with his jaw set.

'Where were you?' he asks.

'Thought I'd teach you a little lesson.'

'What did I do? Nothing!'

'I told you to chuck that old thing.' Kev indicates the hat.

'You can't make me. It's my favourite hat.'

Chook holds on to the precious hat more tightly, checking to see if his girlfriend's name has washed off. Amber. It's still there, though much fainter, with the B almost gone. He remembers when she wrote it. They went on a school excursion to Coffs, with lunch at Macca's, and up the back of the bus on the way home she grabbed his hat and wrote her name in blue biro. Her little brother Luke teased them, but she sat on him and pulled his hair till he screamed for mercy and Mrs Moran had to stop the bus and sort it out.

Kev laughs.

'Suit yourself. Only put it in the back and don't wear it around me. It still fuckin stinks.'

Chook gets out and puts the hat in the back. They leave Macca's and drive round to the train station. It must double as a bus station because Chook sees lots of empty bus bays out the front and two buses pulled up with their doors closed tight. Kev tells Chook he's going to find out when the bus leaves for Broken Hill.

Chook doesn't answer. He watches his dad walk across towards the station entrance and disappear inside. He reaches into his pocket and feels all the cars once more to make sure none of them got left behind at Macca's. They're all there. He relaxes a little as he sees his dad walking back, his shoulders hunched forward as usual and his face looking weary. He gets into the ute and starts the engine without speaking.

'Broken Hill,' says Chook, to break the ice. 'Have I been there?'

'Nope. I was born there.'

'Is the hill really broken?'

'The hill is totally gone.'

'What happened to it?'

'They mined it.'

His dad tells him their bus leaves at 2.15 in the afternoon and gets into Broken Hill at 10.45 that night. Chook groans. It's going to be one of those days that last a lifetime. There are hours to go before they can even get on the bus. They drive round the broad, empty streets of the town, Kev cursing all the roundabouts, new since he was here last, because they slow you down. Chook's impressed at how his dad knows his way round heaps of places, only they keep changing the rules on him.

Almost nothing is open because it's Sunday. Chook eyes off an arcade with a cinema that looks like it might open soon, but his dad says they can't go in there.

'You don't want every bugger in town seeing us. We've got to lie low and not shoot our mouths off or they'll remember us later.'

Chook doesn't know why that's a problem. People always remember his dad later, because he's a top street fighter, even though he never works out. Most people he's hit deserved what they got but Max didn't. Even if he does still owe his dad the money. Chook pushes Max out of his mind again. He mustn't think about him. They park opposite the post office, where four telephone boxes line up like soldiers keeping guard over the building.

Kev reckons it's too early to call Maryanne. He says it would be half an hour earlier in Broken Hill because they keep South Australian time, although they are on the New South Wales side of the border. That doesn't make any sense to Chook.

'Who's Maryanne? Is she one of our family?' he asks.

'Our family! Nah! None of them live there no longer. Anyway, you know what happened to my family, such as it was.'

'Tell me again, Dad . . .'

'Tell you what?'

'About your dad coming in with the hunting rifle and stealing you and your little sisters from your mum.'

Chook has heard this story heaps of times. About Kev's mum getting down behind the bed with her

new boyfriend, the three kids trapped between the
two of them, the little ones screaming, Kev's dad
putting the rifle butt to his mum's head, the kids being
herded away, the late-night ride in the back of a
ute with his sisters and him rolling around like
tumbleweed, the arrival at their dad's house and all
sleeping together in a strange bed, their dad saying
they'd be with him from now on. That didn't last long.
He found the little girls too hard to manage and sent
them over to their granny in Wilcannia on the mail
truck. She sent them back the same way. Kev never
saw them again because they ended up in homes. He
kept Kev with him because he was six years old and
could look after himself.

Kev is not in the mood for storytelling at the
moment. He says: 'I got no time for any of my family.
They wouldn't piss on you if you was burning. Nah,
Maryanne's an old girlfriend of mine.'

Chook isn't surprised. His dad has had heaps of
girlfriends. Girls like him because he makes them laugh
and he's good-looking. It's OK until they move in.
Then the trouble starts. Like with Dianne. She used to
shout in his dad's face until he had to hit her. Chook
has bad memories of those fights. He hopes this
Maryanne isn't a shouter.

'I met her when I was in Boronia,' his dad goes on.
'She was a teacher in there.'

Chook knows his dad was in prison a long time ago, before he was born, though he's not sure what for. Dianne started to tell him once when his dad was outside the shack talking to Huey, but she shut up when he walked back in. She said that's why they ran after that trouble in the pub. That must be why they're running now.

Kev turns on the car radio and Kylie comes on. 'On A Night Like This', the same as the last time they went on the run. How weird is that? Chook joins in, singing in a tuneless shout. Usually Kev sings along too but he isn't in a singing mood this morning. He flicks off the radio.

'Can it!' he says. 'You're making my head hurt.'

Great, thinks Chook. What is he supposed to do now? He looks across towards the post office and sees a young boy coming along the empty street, smoking. He's wearing a red cap, baggy pants, a long-sleeved windcheater and good runners, and can't be much older than Chook. As he gets close to the post office, he looks behind him quickly and then all around, but doesn't see Chook watching. He flicks away his smoke and stops momentarily to look in the little side garden, barely breaking his stride. He's found something that he slips up his sleeve. Chook nudges his dad, who's watching too.

'Could be his dope stash or maybe a blade,' his dad says. 'Cops stop kids and search them all the time now.'

Chook says: 'Shit!' and checks his pocket for his Swiss army knife, hoping the cops don't find that. He's never been searched, yet. The cops have never even questioned him. They started to once but his dad stepped in and told them to leave him alone. They did, too. They'd better not take his knife off him. It was a present from Max for helping him with the sheep.

'Don't swear,' his dad says, cuffing him over the head.

The boy pulls his sleeve down over his hand to cover whatever he scored in the bushes and, pulling his cap down, begins to walk back the way he came. Kev starts the car and moves off too, as if following the boy, who spins round to face them. When he sees they're not cops, he relaxes and turns away.

They go round a corner, brightened by a pub with a balcony painted acid green, and come to a courthouse and a big cop shop with a police car parked outside. XDD 539, the one Axeface and the Boulder were driving, Chook remembers. No sign of them now. They'll be inside, scoffing their takeaways.

They go further along the street, passing an RSL club, which is still shut. They couldn't go in anyway. His dad has been thrown out of too many of those sort of clubs.

Kev drives round the block and under the train line, searching till he finds an out-of-the-way side street. He parks near a flour mill, which even at that hour of the morning is already steaming and hissing away, with smoke coming out of its chimneys. Out the window on Chook's side there's a sign with a picture of a guard dog on it and beneath the sign a real cat is curled up asleep. Chook would like to pat it but when he goes to get out, Kev puts a warning hand on his arm and says: 'Stay here.'

Kev turns off the engine, shuts his eyes and rests his head back. Chook watches him for a while. He isn't sleepy. A little way away, he can see the station lying quiet and empty. He gets out two of his cars and starts to move them around on his knees. A few brrm brrms too many and Kev is irritated.

'Shut up! I'm trying to get some sleep. Get in the back if you want to fuckin play.'

Chook gets in the back, noticing the cat doesn't stir when he opens the door and clambers up onto the tray. It's not much of a guard cat, that's for sure. He sprawls flat out with his cars and the dinosaur head he got at Macca's. He wonders how long it will take to collect the whole dinosaur. With his luck, he'll get all but one leg and they'll change to something different. He'll be left with a dinosaur that can't stand up.

He peeps in at his dad. Kev is lying along the front seat and seems to be asleep. Chook rolls over and looks up into the blue sky. The wind has dropped and the day holds its breath as if waiting for a signal to begin. Clouds drift by like tiny seahorses. Or question marks.

Chook holds the white Mustang convertible Max gave him up to the light.

'I'm sorry about Max,' he whispers. 'Don't let him die.'

The little car glitters back at him. He spins its wheels so they whirr. His stomach grumbles. Now he's hungry. He hopes his dad will let him go back to Macca's for lunch. He knows how fast they run out of good toys.

He thinks about Dianne and Amber, both up in the Nambucca Valley, though not together. His dad can't ever go back there, but he certainly could. He could drive his Mustang all through the day and all night until he got there. Amber would write her name on his hat again and Dianne would hug him and say: 'Great to see you, kiddo!'

Dianne was trying to blow out all the twenty-nine candles on her birthday cake in one go without burning her hair, which stuck out from her head in wild red curls. She got twelve of them out and let Chook do the rest. It took him two goes. Thin smoke curled from the red candles and wax dripped down onto the chocolate icing that Chook had helped her mix in the afternoon. The best part was licking the creamy bowl after he'd got most of it off with the spoon. Chocolate chip cake, heavy on the choc chips, decorated with a striped tiger's head, Dianne's favourite animal. Dianne was good at art, the only thing she liked at school, she said.

They'd got their place on Max's farm pretty well cleaned up by then. They found more rats inside than possums and Dianne and he both hated the huntsman spiders that hung out up near the ceiling, but it would do for now. Neither he nor Dianne wanted to stay long. They wished his dad would get his money so they could split and go back up north where it was warm.

He and his dad sang 'Happy Birthday' and 'Why Was She Born So Beautiful', and when she cut the cake, the knife came out dirty. Chook was the closest boy, so she should have kissed him, but she kissed his dad instead. It went on for too long and Chook saw they were doing that business with their tongues. He was hanging on to her hand but she'd forgotten him. Still kissing her, his dad steered her into the bedroom, breaking Chook's hold, and he saw them fall on top of one another on the bed.

The door stayed open, so Chook saw him pull up her T-shirt, exposing a red bra, then a brown breast. He saw his dad's other hand move to the zipper of her jeans before his dad turned, caught him watching and shoved the door closed with his foot.

Chook cut a big piece of birthday cake, avoiding the tiger's head, and ate it. He was watching TV when she came whirling out of the bedroom later, in the red bra and a pair of not-matching knickers, and swept him up and kissed him, though he tried to pull away. He told her to get some clothes on, but she said it was a bikini, then whizzed over to the CD player, put on Kylie's 'I Should Be So Lucky' and pulled Chook round the floor, dancing in a lucky-lucky-it's-my-birthday way, spinning him round so hard he fell over and lay there laughing.

His dad came out of the bedroom and stood watching, smiling and swaying, cradling a half-empty bottle of beer like a dance partner. 'Lucky, lucky, lucky,' she sang, as she and Chook danced round every square inch of the room like maniacs.

She'd played Kylie on the drive south from the Valley too, the three of them bopping in their seats all night long, his dad glad to get out of the town and hit the road again. Dianne didn't tell them at the truck stop where she worked that she was leaving, just got in the car with his dad and him and took off. She never even asked them where they were going or why. She put her trust in his dad and him. 'On a night like this,' Kylie sang to them then, almost a year ago.

The song finished as his dad hacked off a big slab of birthday cake, cutting fair and square through the tiger's eye and smashing its jaw as well. Dianne got angry.

'Hey, take it from the edge.'

'Too late,' he said, his mouth full.

Chook smoothed over the icing with the knife, trying to reshape the tiger's face, but it was ruined. Dianne cried.

His dad said: 'What did you expect? Did you want to hang it on the wall?'

'I wanted you to leave it for a bit longer,' she said.

Chook went and put Kylie on again but it didn't help. Dianne slammed off into the bedroom, banging the door behind her. Kev looked at Chook and shrugged.

'Women,' he said.

CHAPTER THREE

THE BUS JOURNEY

The bus driver is so fat his legs look like stalks holding up a pumpkin. He sells them tickets to Broken Hill without looking at them and tells them to sit anywhere. The bus is old, with furry purple seats that groan when you lay them back and seat belts you have to sneak up on if you want to pull them out. Neither of them put their belts on, but Chook manages to pull his out to see how far it will go.

It's a relief for both of them to be going somewhere, anywhere, after hours of boring waiting in Dubbo. The highlight was lunch, a Big Mac for his dad and a Happy Meal for Chook. He ate it all this time. His dad didn't want to go back to the same place but Chook begged, holding up the dinosaur head. It was a disappointment, though. He got another dinosaur head. Chook tried to change it but the girl said that was all they had. No legs. No bodies. No tails. It sucked seriously. It was the same girl, Lindy, and she gave his dad a dirty look and threw his change at him.

'Why's she got her knickers in a knot?' his dad asked.

He reminded his dad why. It was because he'd played that trick on him in the car park.

His dad shrugged and said: 'She can mind her own fuckin beeswax.'

Their seats are up the back of the bus, near a young Koori couple and two children. One of the girls is huge and has blonde hair, but the other three, counting the parents, are very small with smooth, dark skin. Chook wonders how the big girl got into that family. A bulky fair-haired man follows them down the back and sits near them, although there are plenty of other spare seats. Chook sees his dad checking the man out and decides he'll keep an eye on him too, in case he's a cop. He's got that cop shape and size, but so far he hasn't given them the usual once-over.

Gradually the front fills up with old people, who rattle on to each other about Jean and Jack, bootscooting and cheap slacks while they wait for the bus to leave. The driver closes the luggage compartment and hauls himself aboard and into his special seat. The bus coughs and chokes but eventually heaves itself off and they head north-west out of Dubbo. The driver tells them his name is Shane and lists all the places they'll be going through on the way. It sounds like an awful lot to Chook: Narromine, Trangie, Nevertire, Nyngan, Hermidale, Boppy Mountain ... there are more, but Chook stops listening.

Kev is silent, looking out the window away from Chook. He tried twice to ring Maryanne before they left Dubbo.

'She's still not there,' he told Chook. 'I keep getting a damn machine that says: "You've rung Maryanne Kelly." I know I've rung Maryanne Kelly, for fuck's sake. Then it goes on like: "I can't get to the phone to take your call," or something, "but if you leave a message I'll get back to you as soon as I can." Fuck me dead. As if I want to talk to a machine.'

'But she still lives there?' Chook asked.

'Yeah. Lucky, eh. I think she's a teacher at the high school. Or she was. The last time I seen her musta been five years ago. I come through Broken Hill on a truck on the way back to Adelaide. You was staying with Les down there. Do you remember Les?'

'I think I remember his dog.'

'Yeah, Rasta.'

Chook remembered Rasta only too well. He was chucking sticks to it in the yard one morning when it went funny. It started making lip-smacking noises, then its back legs suddenly went limp and it fell down, frothing at the mouth. Its legs and its whole body were shaking. When it started weeing everywhere, Chook ran away, screaming that the dog was dying, and somebody, it must have been Les, a man with red whiskers, came and told him the dog was only having a fit. Chook kept right away from Rasta after that.

'She said "I" can't get to the phone, not "we". That's a good sign at least,' Kev went on. 'I'd feel as welcome as a fart in a space suit if she was living with somebody. She'll put us up, no worries, if she can. She's a bloody good woman. Still stuck on me last time I seen her.'

'How do you know?' Chook asked him.

'Trust me, mate, I know. I lived with her for two years once but it didn't work out. She kept trying to change me. She wanted me to go to uni when I got outta can, but I took one look at the campus and run a mile. They all had nappy rash, dead set. None of them had tatts for a start, unless they had them ones you can't see.'

Chook looks at his dad's tatts now. They are as familiar to him as his dad's nose or the smell of his feet. On his forearm he's got a mermaid, with a naked top. Chook likes to trace her blue outline. When his dad tightens his muscles, the mermaid's tail twitches. His dad's knuckles shout out FUCK to the world. He's got a spider's web wrapped around his elbow, with the spider squatting right on the bone. Chook knows what tattoo he's going to get as soon as he's old enough. A red Ferrari with wings and the words 'Eat my dust!' along the side panel.

'She's got to come home some time. She's probably just away for the weekend.'

Chook wonders where they'll stay if she doesn't come home, but knows better than to ask. His dad's bound to have another plan up his sleeve, anyway. He can still hear the old people swapping gossip and prices, with the driver, Shane, joining in over his shoulder as the bus lurches on. A huge black cloud seems to follow them, finally dumping its rain on them just as they pull into the first town up the road, Narromine.

The rain spits on the windscreen and then changes tack, driving low and hard against the sides and windows of the bus, as two passengers get off and make a dash for a shelter shed with some graffiti inside that looks interesting: a drawing of the Koori flag, with words below that Chook asks his dad to read out to him. Kev reads: 'Koori Rulzon ... the only way to play, the only bet is on ... BLACK!' Chook says it over to himself a few times, not quite understanding it, but liking the sound.

When the bus grinds back into action, Chook pulls out his cars and studies them all again. The black Chevvy Corvette is one he got in a swap with Tait

Moran. Tait wanted a Triumph sports car that Chook never liked. The Chevvy is a 1995 Pace car, with a red stripe and the word CORVETTE on the windscreen. He knows his dad likes Corvettes so he turns to show him the wheel bulges on it, but Kev is now leaning back in the reclining seat with his eyes shut. Chook thinks he looks younger with his beard gone and his hair short. He looks like he needs taking care of. Chook touches the leather wristband his dad is wearing, lightly, so he doesn't wake him up. It's a woven strap, with special Navaho Indian beads in the middle. Chook has a matching one he wears round his ankle because his wrist is too thin. They lived for a while with a woman called Willow in a tepee up near Lismore and she made them. They've worn them ever since and, though Willow left a long time ago, he and his dad will stick together forever. That's what the leather bands mean.

He takes a peep across the aisle at the two girls. They stare back at him and one pulls a face and sticks out her tongue. Chook reddens and looks away from their giggles. They should know his great grandmother was Koori too. He's never met her or any of his relatives but his dad has told him. He's taught him all about Mother Earth and told him lots of Dreamtime stories. Like the one about the waratah turning red from the blood of a black snake. Bet they don't know that story.

The snake is his own totem, his dad told him. That's why they never had any trouble from snakes when they slept out amongst them in the bush and on riverbanks. Kev wanted to call him Tai after the taipan but his mum got in first and named him Douglas. Douglas! What a nerdy name. Nobody ever called him that. His dad has called him Chook for as long as he can remember. Something about him panicking and running round like a chook with its head chopped off. Not that he does.

Out of the bus window Chook sees trees and bare paddocks, phone towers on the tops of round hills and tufty grass by the side of the road. The bus rocks and plunges on, and the rain keeps bashing at it, forcing Shane to slow down. He feels his dad wake up with a jerk as the brakes go on, just as they are going past a farm full of broken down caravans, some lying on their side. Chook points them out to his dad. It's just what they need, a van of their own. Kev smiles and shakes his head.

'Not at the moment, mate.'

Fierce clouds are split by lightning. Kev takes a deep breath and says to Chook: 'Nothing beats the smell of fresh rain!'

The next stop, Trangie, looks the same as the last, with the same kind of pub and the same wheat silos. More old ladies get off.

His dad goes up to Shane and asks: 'Can I get off for a smoke?'

'Not until we get to Nyngan, mate. That's the next long stop.'

Kev sits down again, putting away the smoke he's rolled, and mutters 'fuckin arsehole' as he shuts his eyes. Gradually the rain stops and the rhythm of the bus, which seems to eat up the road in steady gulps, makes Chook drowsy. He comes instantly awake though when the radio crackles into action, telling their driver a wide load is coming. Shane pulls well over, onto the soft shoulder of the narrow road, to let the load pass. A tip-truck painted yellow, like a monster toy, slips past on the back of a prime mover, a vision from one of Chook's good dreams. Chook says: 'Cool' and his dad wakes up but he's too late to see it. Kev puts his hand on Chook's head feeling his sharp quills and says: 'Christ, I done a good job of mowing this, eh?' Chook moves his head away, as the driver announces they are coming into Nyngan. His dad says through a yawn that he must have slept through Nevertire, then he laughs.

Chook looks out to see a brown river lapping the top of its banks, as if it will overflow onto the little rickety bridge they are crossing. The bridge is making that kerclunk kerclunk noise that he remembers from up round the Arms, where they were forever crossing old wooden bridges, some with half their planks missing. The river up there, the Nambucca, splits into three arms, North, South and Taylor's, and there are heaps of creeks round, so you're always going over water. His dad used to try to scare him by telling him that trolls lived under the bridges, but no troll could be scarier than his dad. Anyway, the bridges were so low that it would only be a real midget troll that lived there.

'Are we near Broken Hill now?'

'Nowhere near,' Kev says. 'Nyngan's closer to Bourke. I lived here for a while with my dad after we left my mum. Till he had a blue with somebody and we had to move on. Nice town. Gets big floods. They do a lot of sandbagging.'

Chook doesn't know what sandbagging is. It sounds like something he'd like to do, though. One of the schools he went to when he was little had a big sandpit and a digger machine, with levers that let you scoop up shovelfuls of sand and swivel them round, dumping them in another spot. You'd need a machine like that for sandbagging. That's the kind of thing he wants to do when he grows up. Drive one of those big diggers or dump-trucks. He always stops to watch when a truck tips up its tray: the rear flap opens and a load of cement or sand slides out in a great steaming pile. He'll do that, if he can't be a racing car driver.

The bus pulls up in a side street near a closed-up train station. All the stops so far have been outside closed-up stations, Chook has noticed. There is a big crowd waiting as the bus door opens to let Kev and Chook off, but they turn out to be waiting for arriving passengers. Only one new passenger gets on, a young Koori man who looks just like the others on the bus. Chook wonders if he's a relative.

Kev puffs furiously at the smoke he rolled two towns ago, while Chook runs his cars along the footpath in front of a military helicopter that's earthbound there, its propellers wired still. Shane waddles along the side of the bus, removing and adding bags to the luggage compartment. Chook sees the big blond man watching them through the window. He stares back at him, forcing him to look away. If he is a cop, they're in deep shit already. Chook looks up at his dad to see if he is worried, but Kev is walking up and down with a don't-talk-to-me face.

Shane finally slams the luggage doors down and, checking his watch, nods to Chook and his dad. Kev takes a long, last drag, then he, Chook and the driver get back on.

Only eight passengers are left, most of them Koori. Now they leave shops and houses behind as the horizon stretches away forever over deep red soil. Chook sees Kev beginning to relax. This is the country he came from, he tells Chook. This is home.

Chook knows his dad never had a real home, at

least not one with a roof and no wheels. Chook's never had one either, though he's come close from time to time.

'Cobar will be the next place,' Shane wheezes through the microphone, their dinner stop, a couple of hours away. With a solid core of Broken Hill-bound passengers, he puts on the first video: *Dumb and Dumber*. Chook perks up. He likes Jim Carrey. His dad watches it too, though they've both seen it heaps of times. Chook's favourite part, where the cop drinks real piss out of a beer bottle, makes the whole bus laugh. Chook watches the blond man out of the corner of his eye. He's laughing too, so maybe he's not a cop. The video finishes just as they come into a town.

'Cobar,' his dad says.

Chook looks out to see pools of muddy water lying on the road and filling up a dam his dad says was left behind by an old mine.

Cobar is hot and fly ridden even at 6.30 p.m. Chook is starving. He tumbles out of the bus and heads for the roadhouse before he realises his dad has stopped for a smoke with the two Koori blokes, who look like twins, same height, same skinny build, same faces. The three of them chat easily as they smoke, his dad about a head taller than the other two.

Chook's stomach is complaining. He hops from foot to foot. When, finally, his dad slips the butt into his butt bag and comes over to him, Chook says: 'I thought you said we weren't allowed to talk to anyone.'

'Hey! Don't get cheeky. Koori people are OK. They'd never give you up.'

They go into the roadhouse and Chook chooses a hamburger with chips, wolfing them down when they come. They notice the big blond man is about to make light work of two pies and a sausage roll. Kev says he isn't hungry. He spots a phone and goes to dial Maryanne's number. Chook sees him bending his head, listening. Then he slams down the phone without speaking and heads back to Chook.

'Same fuckin machine.'

'What'll we do, Dad?'

'Nothing we can do. We're on our way now. She's got to come home eventually. If she's not there when we arrive, maybe we'll break in. She'll understand.'

Chook hopes so. There have been a lot of people in their lives who haven't understood.

'There might be a dog,' he warns his dad. 'An Alsatian or a pit bull . . .'

Kev is good with dogs, so is Chook, if they don't take fits, but ones that are trained to kill are another story. When Chook was little, they had a pure-bred Rottweiler, Samson, that went everywhere with him. People reckon Rotties are savage, but Samson always took good care of him. Chook would like another one like that. They don't get caught down holes because they're too big, they can't jump high because they're too heavy and they stick by you.

When they step outside the roadhouse, the air is hot and heavy, as if a storm has just passed. A young girl with a baby in a pram goes by, calling out to somebody across the road. Chook wishes they were in Broken Hill now. He feels like he's been travelling long enough.

The others have already got back onto the bus. The driver puts on *Batman*. Chook follows the other kids and one of the Koori men down the front for a better view. As kilometre upon kilometre zooms by and the western sky darkens, Batman flies around Gotham City in his Batmobile and Chook forgets he's going nowhere fast.

There is one more stop after *Batman* finishes, a toilet-and-drinks stop in the fading light, at a roadhouse outside Wilcannia. All the men chat together over smokes as Shane waddles into the roadhouse. The minute he vanishes, the men open the luggage compartment and get out their bags. Soon cans of beer are being passed round. Even the blond man, who's kept himself separate up to now, is part of it, Chook notices.

He ignores the girls before they ignore him and starts chucking rocks at the toilet block until he gets bored with that and runs his cars round a track he sets up in the dirt.

This time he's Prost driving the Porsche. He's in the lead when he gets engine trouble. Quick, into the pit stop for repairs. He sees Schumacher steam by, sneering, the big cheat. He's out of the pit now and chasing him. For once, luck is on his side. Schumacher rolls on the last bend and the Porsche goes through and takes the chequered flag. Hooray! Prost wins! They're putting the wreath around his neck and he's fizzing the champagne everywhere when he sees Max watching in the crowd. He isn't cheering. He turns and walks away. Chook calls: 'Max! Max!' But he vanishes.

Shane is angry when he comes back. Apparently the luggage compartment is his territory and is not to be touched. He claims it's because of security but Kev says it's got more to do with the bus company's ban on beer.

'He's a racist pig,' he says, as Shane bangs the doors down extra loudly. The men finish their beers and get back on the bus for the final leg to Broken Hill.

They stop briefly in Wilcannia to let the big blond man off.

'Cop!' Kev whispers to Chook after he passes.

Chook says: 'I knew it. That's why I've been keeping an eye on him. Has he been following us?'

'Nah, off duty. I thought at first he might be but he's just coming back to work from time off.'

It's as dark as a wild dog's den for the last hour into Broken Hill. Chook puts his head down on Kev's lap, feeling Kev stroking his hair as he drops off to sleep.

Chook and his dad are walking through some town that looks a bit like Bowraville, it's got big old wooden houses and verandahs, when this humungous dog comes straight at them out of a yard with grass growing up to the top of the fence. Chook can just see a blur of black, snapping teeth and red eyes. It's on top of them, and he's screaming 'it hurts, it hurts' and he can hear his screams all mixed up with the dog's snarls and his dad's shouts and threats. The sky's gone dark and there's only pain and noise and scaredness.

Lucky his dad's got a knife: he pulls it out and shoves it straight into the dog's throat. The dog starts to make these kind of strangled sounds and he hears his screams die away. It flops down in front of them and his dad kicks it and says: 'That's what you've got to do with wild dogs, go for the throat with your bush knife. It stops them dead in their tracks.'

Chook can't take his eyes off the blood that's still pouring from the hole in the dog's neck and, while he's watching, its whole body shakes violently one last time. His dad asks if he's all right but he doesn't know yet. He can't feel anything.

CHAPTER FOUR

BROKEN HILL

Broken Hill is dead quiet at eleven o'clock, the night mild and spotty with stars, when the bus pulls into Crystal Street outside the train station. Shane hasn't recovered from the raid on his luggage compartment. He yanks their bags out from under the bus and flings them down on the footpath. Before they can pick them up, he bangs down the doors, gets back on the bus and drives away without looking back at them. The Koories gather up their stuff and disappear into the night.

Barely awake, Chook stands blinking at his bag, until his dad tells him to pick it up and get going. It's a scary feeling, walking through an unknown town in the middle of the night. Usually they're driving when they come to a new place. If only they still had Max's ute. His dad said they had to dump it so the cops couldn't track the rego number. Chook knows it was the right thing to do but the street lights are dim and he's exhausted. His dad says they'll be fine now, though he doesn't sound as if he believes it.

'I know the way. Broken Hill's easy to get around, because it's like a big rectangle. We go up Sulphide Street, turn right into Mica, then throw a left into Oxide. Maryanne lives three or four blocks along Oxide Street.'

Three or four blocks! Chook can barely carry his bag one block. His dad takes one side for a while when Chook stumbles. Only one car goes by as they walk, the driver looking at them curiously.

Chook can tell his dad is feeling anxious as they get near Maryanne's house, because he shifts his bag from hand to hand, brushes off his clothes and clears his throat.

'This is it,' he says, stopping suddenly.

The house is in darkness. A street light outside shows them that all the windows are closed. She'll be asleep, of course. They look at each other, then Kev takes a deep breath and they tiptoe up the path and onto the porch. Kev knocks gently at the front door, trying not to wake the neighbours. No dog barks, much to Chook's relief. Kev knocks again, louder, but the knocks fall into a gloomy silence. Chook begins to whine.

'I'm tired, Dad. What are we going to do now? We come all this way for nothing.'

'Shut up!' says Kev.

Chook slumps down on his bag and puts his head on his knees.

'Stay here,' Kev hisses at him and goes round the back of the house. Chook can hear him trying windows and doors. It's hopeless. There's nowhere they can go. Nowhere they belong. He's sick of running away all the time.

He lifts his head in time to see his dad heading over to a garage that's beside the house. He tugs at its roller door, but it doesn't move. Then he tries a little side door, which opens. Chook sees him looking into the blackness inside. He calls softly to Chook to come over but, just as Chook is about to join him, they hear a door open next door and a torch shines first on Chook, then swings round towards Kev.

'Who's there?' a man's voice calls.

As their eyes adjust to the harsh light, they can make out a man's shape, bulky and squat like a gorilla, standing on the porch of the house next door. He holds the torch high with one hand, the other hanging down by his side.

'We're friends of Maryanne Kelly,' Kev says.

'Are you now?'

'We just got off the bus and thought we'd look her up.'

'She's away,' the neighbour says.

'I tried to ring,' Kev says.

'Mmm ...'

'Any idea when she's coming back?'

'Coupla days, maybe.'

'Right. Pity we can't hang round. We're on our way to Adelaide.'

The man keeps his torch on them till they pick up their bags and begin to move off. Then he snaps off the torch and they hear the door shut. Back to his ugly old gorilla wife, Chook thinks savagely.

'Fuck fuck fuck fuck fuck fuck fuck fuck!' he hears his dad grinding between clenched teeth.

Chook knows better than to speak. He wishes he was dead. Nothing ever goes right for him. Wherever he goes he brings bad luck. Whatever gods control general fuck-ups have got it in for him. Shops shut the minute he gets to the door. They always leave town as the swimming pool is opening and arrive as it's closing. Kids get hurt just hanging out with him.

Kev is walking ahead as if he doesn't care whether Chook follows or not. Chook follows because he's got no choice, his legs like jelly.

They walk aimlessly along a side street, the houses all wrapped in darkness, no cars passing. Ahead, the ground stretches away, bare and treeless. There is nowhere to hide. They were better off back on the farm. At least there were trees. Chook's legs ache and his bag feels like it's got bricks in it. If they had a car they could have slept in it. They've lived in plenty of cars in their time. The old Falcon they had up at Taylor's Arm was the best. It had bench seats front and back so he and his dad could both stretch out, and a big boot where they could stash their food away from animals. If the adults had a party, Chook and his mates could get in the car and spy on them or wind the windows up and crash out when they'd seen enough.

Suddenly his dad turns off the footpath and heads across a little park they're passing. It's got no grass, only gravel, and no play equipment, so it's not a real park. More of a vacant block. There are no lights at the back of it, just two seats facing towards each other, a bubbler and a small toilet block that's all locked up. Kev stops and puts his bag on one of the seats. Chook goes to put his bag there too, but his dad snaps at him: 'The other seat. That's yours.'

Chook puts his bag on the other seat and hangs like a hooked fish, waiting for his dad to tell him what to do next. He sees his dad getting his towel and some clothes out of his bag and spreading them along the seat and it dawns on Chook that they are going to sleep right here. He copies his dad, looking in his bag for something to spread along his seat too, but can't seem to find anything long enough. His dad comes over and grabs the clothes off him that he has half

50

spread out and bundles them up to make a pillow for him. Then he brings a long pair of his jeans to put on Chook's seat and helps Chook lie down on them.

The seat is hard but Chook doesn't complain. He's glad to stop at last and grateful for his dad's help. The clothes under his head make a soft pillow. He pulls the cars and his Swiss army knife out of his pockets, because they're lumpy to sleep on, and puts them beside his makeshift pillow. His dad spreads Chook's army camouflage jacket over him. There are no clouds to keep the cold up in the sky and it's now starting to drift down on top of them.

His dad sits down on the end of Chook's seat, squashing Chook's legs up, and reaches into his pocket for rollie paper and tobacco. Chook watches him through half-closed eyes. When Kev has his smoke rolled, he sees him bring the match up to light it, the flame showing his haunted face. He looks as if a bad dream has come true and he needs someone to be there for him in the night.

Chook wriggles closer, puts his hand up and strokes the stubble where his dad's beard used to be. His dad turns his head, pressing Chook's hand wordlessly against his shoulder. Then he takes a long drag and blows the smoke out heavily, looking down at the gravel beneath the seat.

Chook says: 'Dad . . .'

Kev doesn't look at him; just keeps on staring at the ground.

'Dad, why did you and Max ... I mean, what happened when you came home?'

The question has been trembling behind his lips ever since they left the farm, but his dad hasn't looked like he wanted to answer.

There's a pause, then Kev says: 'I can't tell you. Just trust me, mate. I didn't have no choice.'

'Will he be all right?'

This question is even more important but it seems to make his dad mad again. He takes another draw on his smoke and gets up abruptly, going over to his own seat and stretching out, pulling his big jacket over him before he says: 'Of course he will. I only knocked him out. I told you that already. Now, drop it!'

Chook pushes away the memory of Max's body lying on the bed as still as a car wreck and looks up at the millions of stars coming out above him, wrapped in the white ribbon of the Milky Way. Suddenly he sees something brighter moving purposefully across the sky, threading a steady course between the stars. He points it out to his dad. Maybe it's a flying saucer.

'Nah, it's a satellite or some piece of space junk,' his dad says. 'There's tons of satellites up there spying on us. We've got fuckin tribes of them watching our every move from outer space. Someone, somewhere, can probably see you and me right now, lying on these benches.'

Chook sits up straight away in alarm. If that's true, they should keep on running.

His dad says: 'It's OK, Chook. Lie down. I'm exaggerating a bit. They might not be able to see us in the dark. But it's not far off happening, I swear. Even out here in the middle of nowhere.'

Chook checks all around before he lies back down again. He can't see any sign of life, though cyber spies could be beaming signals down to some cop shop right now. His dad keeps smoking calmly, so he can't be too worried.

They both saw a real flying saucer once up near Huey's shack at Taylor's Arm. It came flashing fast towards them and then turned side on so they could see the saucer shape and what looked like heads in little windows, before it zoomed off again. Nobody believed them but the two of them definitely saw it and his dad wasn't stoned either. Another time he was climbing on the Falcon's bonnet about twilight when he saw a huge drawing in the sky, like the outline of a person, with a body, two legs and arms and a big round head. It was all outlined in pink swirly light. He called to his dad but he was making out with Dianne, and by the time he came out all that was left was the light slowly fading.

When he told his dad what he'd seen, his dad said maybe it was God. Chook didn't know if he was joking, though. He's never seen God again anyway, if that's who it was.

He turns to watch his dad, who's still smoking steadily and looking up at the sky. Chook wonders what he's thinking about.

'Were you born near here, Dad?'

'Dunno. Once me and my dad left, we never come back. I got no idea where I was born. Could have been in the hospital. Or down some creek bed more likely.'

'What was your dad doing here?'

'Truck driving, I think. That's what he mostly done. That or dozer driving. My dad could drive anything on wheels.'

Like I'm going to, Chook thinks proudly.

'He'd travel round doing grading and stuff for the shire. We usually stayed in a caravan and he'd go away, sometimes days at a time, working on the roads. I'd be left alone in the van. Once I burnt myself real bad. I was swinging a billy of boiling water round my head like the old bushies do, when it went all over my arm. I had to make up this sort of paste of gum leaves to take the heat out of it, you know, like I do for you. I musta only been about seven then. Pretty smart kid, eh?'

Chook's dad uses bush remedies he learnt from his own father on Chook all the time. Some of them hurt more than what they're supposed to fix, but they do work. Eventually.

'Did your dad get another wife?'

'My dad had hundreds of women but no more wives, no. He used to bring chicks home to the caravan and get me out of bed to recite the Lord's Prayer.'

'What's that?'

'Something we was taught to say before we went to sleep. It goes: "Our Father which art in Heaven…" That's the way it starts, any rate. I think that was how he felt when he was pissed. Like he was in heaven. Me, I'd be left wide awake in the dark afterwards, listening to him and some woman making out.'

That's happened to Chook often enough but he doesn't say anything or his dad will get mad again.

'And where's your dad now? I never met him, have I?'

'Dunno where he is and I don't care. I never bothered with him since I left home. We had a blue and I cleared out. I wouldn't mind finding me sisters one day but I don't know where to start. They probably got married and changed their names.'

'Did your mum ever come looking for you and your sisters?'

'Nah. Never seen her again. She was a piece of shit, I told you.'

Like his own mum, Chook thinks. It's funny how his dad and his dad's dad can't find good women. Or when they find them, they can't keep them.

'Where are we going next, Dad? Adelaide?'

'I just told that prick Adelaide to put him off the scent.'

His dad has another drag on his smoke and blows it out heavily again.

'I ain't decided yet. I'm sort of inclined to stick around till Maryanne gets back. That prick said a coupla days . . .'

'Will Maryanne help us?'

'Course she will. She'd do anything for me.'

'Are you sure?'

'Yep. Sure I'm sure. She owes me. I reckon she still feels bad about dumping me so fast. She fell for me like a ton of bricks when she was my teacher but when I come outta the can, she couldn't go through with it. Dropped me like a hot potato. I didn't fit in with her furniture or her fine wines or her fine fuckin friends.'

'What did she used to teach you, Dad?'

'Maths. I was her best student. I passed my uni entrance exams with her. Mature age entry, any rate. Not bad for a bushy who's hardly been to school. What's the point, though? Nobody's going to give me a chance. I found that out. They take one look at the tatts and the face and they make up their minds straight away about me. All they got to do is give me some space, some respect, but they can't do that. People have to fuckin push me. Then they get what's coming to them and they don't like it. People shit me, they really do.'

His dad is working himself up with every word but Chook is only half listening. He's heard his dad say all this often before. He feels his eyes closing, in spite of the hard seat and the cold, when there is a little noise at his side and something furry touches him. He looks down. A ginger cat is rubbing against his seat, its tail brushing his hand. He reaches down and pats it, hearing its miaou turn into a purr.

'Look, Dad,' he says.

Kev looks over and says: 'Where's my gun when I need it?'

Chook holds the cat closer against the seat as if to protect it. Kev says cats kill native animals, but that's only feral ones. This cat is somebody's pet. Chook likes the way cats twist and twine themselves around you. Dogs are better, of course, if you want to play, but cats adopt you. He strokes the cat, feeling it bend to his touch, its whole back curving in time with his stroking. He pats the seat beside him and the cat jumps up, curling itself alongside him, lying snugly on his cars and his Swiss army knife. He can feel it warming him up, its whole body vibrating, as he tucks it closer still.

His dad finishes his smoke and turns over on his side, facing Chook, wriggling to try to get comfortable. He cocks his finger like a trigger at the cat, but he's only joking.

'Night, Chook,' he says. 'Try and get some zeds. We'll get up before dawn and take a closer look at the town. See if there's anywhere we can hide out till Maryanne gets back.'

Chook says good night to his dad and feels sleep stealing towards him. The cat licks his face. He wishes he could keep it forever. He's had to say goodbye to too many pets. Apart from Samson and Twitch, there was a ferret called Nosy that he used to wear round his neck and up his shirt, till it went missing one night while he slept. He's always wondered if his dad had something to do with that. His dad doesn't like ferrets either.

His dad, of all people, should understand how it feels to lose a pet. Kev told him once that when he was a kid he lost a dingo pup he was trying to tame because his father said they couldn't take it with them. He watched his father go for a walk with the pup and a rifle and come back with just the rifle. Kev said he was always worried afterwards that his father would suggest taking him for a walk.

★ ★ ★

Max is laughing the way he always does when you tickle him. He laughs himself sick. He specially hates being tickled on his feet, so Chook is trying to get hold of one and Max is swinging his legs round, barely keeping them out of reach, when he falls off the bed. Plop, onto the floor, his thin bits of hair surprised into life, his legs waving in the air like a dying cockroach. Now Chook is the one laughing, looking down at his shocked face.

Before Max can get up, Chook jumps on top of him and they roll over and over, wrestling and tickling. They only stop when they're totally pooped from too much laughing. Max is wheezing like an old train going up a hill.

Chook is still lying on top of Max when he looks down and sees that Max's eyes are starting to roll back in his head. All he can see is the whites of them. He freaks out and tries to escape, tries to push himself away, but Max has got him. His fingers feel bony and strong like a skeleton's digging into his back. He can't get away, no matter how he wriggles. He starts punching him, shouting at him to let him go and whacking him as hard as he can.

CHAPTER FIVE

MOSQUE

There's someone shaking him and mumbling like a crazy man, smelling of stale piss and beer. Chook opens his eyes. It's not his dad. It's someone he doesn't know, leaning over him, muttering. He shouts out to his dad and tries to push the man away, his heart thumping. He can only dimly make him out in the dark. The man is slurring words Chook can't understand, almost crying, his breath stinking. Next minute his dad is up and pulling the man off him and onto the ground.

'What the fuck . . .'

Chook's dad gets out a torch from his bag and shines it down. Its light picks out an old dero, lying tumbled in a bundled heap, still yelping, his bags scattered, his moist eyes looking at his dad pleadingly.

'What do you think you're doing?' his dad asks, softer once he sees the man is harmless.

'It's my seat,' the man whines. 'This is my spot.'

Chook sits up slowly, still shaking, wrapping his coat round himself, and watches his dad help the man pick up his scattered bags.

'That's cool, fella,' his dad says. 'We gotta go anyway. Come on, Chook. We'll give him his seat.'

It's still dark and Chook doesn't want to budge. He sees his dad turn away and begin to put his clothes in his bag as the old man gets slowly to his feet. Kev looks at Chook again.

'Come on,' he says, 'hurry up and put your stuff in your bag and we'll go.'

Still fuddled with sleep and bad dreams, Chook gets off the seat and begins to put the clothes back into his bag. His dad's jeans don't belong there though, and the bag bulges and won't do up. Chook is too tired and clumsy to care. He looks round for the cat, which is nowhere in sight. Maybe it turned into the old dero. Cats hang out with witches so they're bound to know a bit of magic. He puts his cars and his knife back in his pockets. The dero is hovering close to him, as if someone else might grab his seat if he doesn't get in first. Chook moves further away from his smell, hearing a rustle of paper, as the man pulls something bottle shaped out of the pocket of his coat.

'What time is it?' he asks his dad. Kev looks at his watch by the torchlight.

'It's half past five in the morning. We've had a few hours' sleep. Good time to leave.'

As Chook and he pick up their bags and start walking off, Chook sees the dero plop down instantly on the seat he's left and take a sip out of his bottle to celebrate. He arranges his bags with practised ease and lies down in the warmth Chook left behind. Chook looks around for the cat one last time, but it's disappeared.

His dad leads off, back the way they came last night, towards Maryanne's. They've only gone a few hundred metres when they see it. A police car, parked outside her house.

Kev grabs Chook's arm to stop him.

'How did they find out so quick?' he hisses.

'That man next door . . .' Chook says.

'We didn't do nothing wrong. He saw us leave the place.'

'Maybe those cops in Macca's told them. Or the guy on the bus?'

Their words tumble out together and run into each other.

'But they weren't following us, were they?'

'That spy satellite, Dad?'

'I don't think so.'

His dad drags him towards the front door of an old shop on the other side of the road. It looks as if it hasn't been a shop since Capstan smokes were on sale, but it has a sort of alcove with a wall to shelter them from the street. Kev puts Chook behind him and peeps round again at the cop car.

'What are they doing at Maryanne's if she ain't there?' he wonders.

'Maybe they've gone into the gorilla's place next door,' Chook says. His dad shakes his head.

'Nobody would know about me and Maryanne. We go back fifteen years and it all happened in South Aus anyway. This is freaking me out, I tell you, Chook.'

Chook pulls at his dad's arm.

'We should get away, Dad. Now! Come one! Before they see us.'

His dad shakes his hand off.

'Just let me think for two minutes, if you don't bloody mind.'

Chook knows thinking is a waste of time. What they need now is action. He jigs up and down, keen to get out of there, but his dad brings his hand down hard on his head, trying to keep him still, absorbed in watching the cop car over the road.

Suddenly he feels the hand on his head go tense. He hears his dad let out a breath.

'What? What is it, Dad?'

'Maryanne . . . it's Maryanne.'

'Is it? Is she there after all? So that gorilla was lying. Or maybe she just got home, Dad. That guy said two days. He must of been trying to —'

Kev puts his hand over Chook's mouth and pulls him forward slightly so he can get a look at what is happening.

He sees a porch light on at Maryanne's house and a man and a woman have come out the front door and are standing on the porch. The man has his arms round the woman and his back to them and is wearing a cop's uniform. The woman he's holding has a coat on and blonde hair but that's all Chook can see, because she is kissing the cop.

'Her boyfriend,' Chook says.

'Fuckin dog.' Kev drags out the words as if he's reading them off something. Her tombstone, maybe.

While they watch, the cop finishes smooching, steps away from her and walks down the path to the gate, opens it, waves, and goes towards his car. Chook has a look at the number plate as the car's lights go on, in case it's one he knows. It's not. Maryanne wraps her coat tight round her and waves back. As the cop gets into his car and drives away, she turns and goes back into the house.

Kev leans his head against the side of the shop window, his eyes shut. Chook wishes he didn't look so lost. He waits, wondering what they'll do now. His dad lifts his head finally and looks at Chook.

'A fuckin cop. I feel like throwing up. I wanted to smash his fuckin window and put my fist in his face. I can't believe she'd do that. Kiss a fuckin cop.'

'Right on the lips. Big wet one,' Chook says.

Kev's body jerks and he puts out his arm as if to shut Chook up. Cops have been the enemy for as long as Chook can remember. Maryanne kissing a cop is about as bad as it gets. It certainly puts them in the shit. But maybe it means they'll move on now. There's nothing here for them.

'We should've let his tyres down, Dad,' Chook says, trying to cheer his dad up.

Kev doesn't answer. Chook sees him pick up his bag and start to walk off, back towards the park, away from Maryanne's house. Chook follows him, the legs of his dad's jeans trailing out of his bag. He's still sleepy. The houses they pass are in darkness, the street lights on, people not even yawning awake yet. As they pass the park again, Chook looks over to where the old man is sleeping on his seat and wishes he had it back.

He follows his dad down the hill till they reach what looks like a main road and then they turn left, Kev setting a furious pace, Chook struggling to keep up. On the edge of town, where the houses stop, Kev suddenly stops too. Chook sees a high wire fence and a padlocked wire gate with a sign on it. Kev steps closer to read the sign. He is peering through the gate down a path lined with what look like date palms when Chook catches up with him.

'What is it?' he asks.

'It says it's an old mosque museum. Closed till further notice.'

'What's that, Dad? A mosque.'

'A kind of church,' says Kev.

On the right-hand side is a bunch of what look like old people's units and on the left, a house with a high side fence. The fence on the units' side is lower and looks easy to climb over. Kev moves to it and throws his bag over.

'Come here,' he whispers to Chook.

'We can't ...' Chook has just enough strength to protest, 'we can't stay in a church.'

'Shut up!' Kev grabs Chook's bag off him and throws it over the fence too, finally dislodging the jeans which fly through the air. Then he gets hold of Chook, thrusting him to the top of the tin fence and watching as he finds his way down the other side, the cars and the Swiss army knife banging against the tin. Kev follows him over easily. They pick up their bags and the jeans and crunch along the gravel to the door of what looks like a big shed. Kev tries it. It's locked. There's a small window to the right of the door and another bigger one to the right of that. His dad has a good go at both of the windows but they're stuck fast.

Chook trails after his dad round the back where they find another smaller shed, standing separate and windowless. Its door is also locked. His dad turns round to the main shed again and sees that it has a back window, which gives slightly when he tugs at it, but stays locked. He gets the torch out of his bag and takes a look at it.

'If I break the top pane I could reach the lock,' he says. 'It's just whether I'll make too much noise.'

He looks round to see if any neighbours are awake. There are no lights on yet. Chook waits without any hope that this will work out. He's losing faith that his dad has any sort of plan, now that Maryanne is out of the picture. He half squashes the jeans back into the bag and sits down on it. He sees his dad get something out of his bag and tap the window firmly.

The glass is old. It gives with a quiet tinkle. Kev listens for a moment. Nothing stirs. He releases the lock and pushes the window up high enough for the two of them to climb in. He sends Chook in first, telling him to be careful of the broken glass. Chook doesn't think he'll notice if the glass cuts him or not. He's tired enough to sleep on the stuff. Once he's in, his dad hands him the two bags and then climbs in himself, banging his head as he comes through and swearing at Chook as if it's his fault. It always is.

It's dark inside and spooky. Chook clings to Kev as they crunch away from the broken glass and then feel something soft under their feet. Kev shines the torch down. They see some small rugs on the floor with a foreign-looking pattern on them. They move through the first room and into a second room, both of them small enough to fit inside one of the classrooms up at his bush school. The torch shows almost no furniture in either room, though the second has pictures on the walls of men in turbans leading camels, and glass cases with more foreign stuff in them.

'Well,' says Kev, 'this looks like where we're staying today.'

It'd better only be for one day. The place smells of dead animals, especially rats, a bit like the farmhouse when they first arrived, and Chook can hear the shuffle of ghostly feet on the floor, maybe some of those dead old camel men in the pictures.

'Dad, why can't we go on now? To Adelaide?'

'Shut the fuck up about Adelaide! Forget Adelaide! I need time to think what we're gunna do now. Everything's changed. The one thing I know for sure is we need to keep out of sight for a while. OK? Trust me!'

Chook goes into the first room, the room with rugs, and flops down onto one of them without speaking. After a while, he sits up, takes off his shoes then lies down again and pulls his army coat over his head. It isn't cold now but the coat comforts him. Dianne bought it for him in Bathurst to make up, after an argument they had. He wears it everywhere, even though it's three sizes too big.

His dad must have followed him in, because he hears him settle down nearby and scrabble in his tobacco pouch, then there's the faint crackle of rollie paper. That's the last thing he hears.

When he raises the coat again to get some air, a couple of hours must have passed, because the sky through the broken window pane is now bright blue and cloudless. He can hear a man's voice nearby, then a little boy's. 'Peter', the man calls the kid.

'Neighbours,' says Kev. 'Too bloody close.'

Maybe that means they won't stay too long. It's already getting hot under the tin roof. Chook looks round the bare room. The walls are green with a pattern of wavy lines stamped into their tin surface. It looks like the sea. In one wall there's a kind of hollow you could stand in, shaped like a coffin tipped on its end, with foreign writing and pictures all round. The dozen or so rugs are laid out in two rows on a red floor. Some are faded as if they've lain there too long.

'Weird kind of church,' he says.

'Why?' asks his dad, a tobacco paper stuck to his bottom lip.

'The one at home had a picture of Mary holding the baby Jesus and a big wooden cross on the wall. Remember?'

'This lot don't believe in Jesus,' his dad says.

'Don't they? But there's not even any seats.'

Max's church stood on a hill near their farmhouse. It had uncomfortable wooden seats, like benches. Max told Chook they were meant to be uncomfortable, so people stayed awake during the priest's sermon. Max only went to church at Christmas or for weddings and funerals and Chook never went, but he crept inside once and tried out the seats.

Kev takes the paper from his lip before he answers. There can't be much tobacco left, because Chook sees him rolling a real skinny one. He doesn't like the look of that. His dad running out of tobacco is bad news.

'They don't sit. They kneel on these rugs to pray. I seen 'em on telly.'

Kev lights the smoke he's rolled and takes a big drag.

'Tell you what, I'd kill for a coffee.'

Chook knows that. He dreads it. Ten years with his dad have taught him he needs two things in the morning and fast: tobacco and coffee, in that order. Without them, he's nasty. Worse, murderous.

'What day is it, Dad?'

'Must be Monday.'

'And what's the time now?'

Kev looks at his watch.

'Ten o'clock.'

'Do you think they'd have found M ...' his name won't come out, 'by now?'

Kev shrugs. 'Probably. Unless he come to by himself and left yesterday.'

Chook thinks there's no way Max could have come to by himself, but he doesn't say so.

His dad goes on: 'Jimmy would have come looking for us this morning and found him.'

Jimmy is a cousin of Max's, two or three times removed, his dad said, which Chook never understood. Where was he removed to or from? And why so often?

Jimmy's been helping Max and Kev with drenching for the last couple of weeks. Max says that he and Jimmy always give each other a hand with big jobs like that. He lives over on the next hill and has been picking them up for work over in the back paddock ever since they totalled the car.

There is an almighty crash outside the back wall. They both freeze for several seconds, then Chook hides under his coat again. There's another smaller crash, then quiet.

Chook peeps out to see his dad creeping over to the back window. There is a long pause.

'What is it?' he whispers to Kev. 'Is it the cops?'

Kev shakes his head and gestures to him to be quiet. They hear a woman's voice talking, then a man's. Then she calls to Peter to hurry up. They hear a door open and close and the voices stop.

Kev stays at the window.

The next thing they hear is a car engine starting up and car doors banging. Then the car reverses out of the driveway and pauses before setting off towards town. The car noise dies away. There's silence.

Kev takes a long drag on his smoke.

'What was it, Dad?'

'They must use this place as a rubbish dump. They've thrown a whole pile of old glass and rusty tin over the fence. They should be bloody ashamed of themselves.'

Kev is a real greenie. He hates people dumping their rubbish. Always has.

'What'll we do, Dad? Report them?'

His dad comes over and hauls him off the rug.

'Get up, smartarse! Let's have breakfast. We got baked beans.'

Cold. Yuck. Instantly Chook isn't hungry.

Kev looks in his bag for the can and the opener, then decides to take the whole bag into the next room. He says it's more civilised to eat away from where they sleep, like a dog doesn't shit near water. Chook doesn't see how it's the same kind of thing. He snuggles down under his coat, avoiding beans.

'Come here,' his dad calls. Chook gets up and shuffles into the next room, rubbing the back of his hand across his nose and sniffing, still wearing Saturday night's clothes.

'Get two plates and a coupla spoons outta there,' his dad says, indicating the bag. 'This ain't a one man show.'

Chook hurries to find them. He knows better than to argue with his dad about helping. He broke Chook's front tooth once when he didn't do his chores. It was a second tooth and now it's got a real jagged edge.

He sets two plastic plates and two spoons out on the old wooden floor. His dad is already opening the can. The smell of the gooey contents turns Chook's stomach.

He walks away and looks in the glass cases. In one, there are clothes: a beautiful gold embroidered vest, some baggy pants, and slippers with toes that curl up. There's a note on the glass that Chook can't read. Reading is something he avoided at the schools he went to. Not that he's stupid, he can certainly read his and Amber's names and stuff like 'the cat sat on the mat'. The trouble was teachers gave you baby books and wanted you to read them aloud while the rest of the class made signs behind your back and called you a dumbo. That's what he liked about Amber. She beat anyone up who did that.

'What does this say?' he asks his dad, desperate to avoid the beans he is spooning onto the two plates.

His dad looks round briefly.

'It says they belonged to a camel driver called . . .' he has to come over with the can in his hand to read the name: 'Shamroze Khan.'

'Is he the owner of this place?'

'Nah. He'd be dead as a dodo. Pushing up daisies. Or gone home. They don't need camels no more. They got trucks.'

'Where's their home?'

'India. Afghanistan. I dunno. They was a bloody long way from home out here, that's for sure. Come on. Breakfast is served.'

Chook reluctantly turns away from a second glass case that's got a camel bell and a peacock feather fan in it. He would like to hear the sound of the bell and to stroke the feathers but Kev is already handing him his plate and spoon.

'Here. Get that into ya.'

Chook feels as if he's going to be sick again. 'I hate cold baked beans.'

'Too bad. Eat 'em. How am I going to cook the bastards?'

Chook can see his point but he can't make the cold slimy things go down his throat.

'Dad,' he says, 'can I get a drink?'

'No.'

'But is there a tap?'

'I bloody well hope so. Now shut up and start eating.'

'Dad . . .'

Kev looks at him warningly.

'I need a piss.' Chook puts the plate down and walks to the door. It's locked.

His father says: 'Eat first.'

'I'll wet my pants. Please, Dad.'

He jigs on the spot.

Kev finally gets up and comes over to the door. He shoves Chook out of the way and reaches up for a key hanging on a hook, which he fits into the ancient lock. As soon as it turns, Chook races outside, looking for a toilet. There isn't one. Kev shrugs and gestures from the doorway towards a date palm.

Chook looks round. There are no cars coming down the street. He pulls down his trackie pants and pees as quickly as he can. When he finishes, he calls to his dad: 'There's a tap out here.'

'Good,' his father says, turning to go back inside.

Chook wants more time. He washes his hands slowly, then has a long drink.

'What's that?' he says, pointing at a heavy wooden thing in the yard.

'An old cart. Camel cart, probably.' Kev turns against his will to look at it. 'Big bugger, ain't it?'

'Yeah!' Chook is already starting to climb on it.

'Get inside and eat. Now!'

Chook knows his time is up. He drops down off the cart, landing in a patch of vicious prickles, and goes back inside, limping. Kev shuts the door and locks it behind him again. The plate of cold baked beans is still lurking on the floor, where Chook left it. He sits down and starts pulling the prickles out of his feet, surprised he can even feel them. He's hardly ever worn shoes except to school, so his feet are tough, but these are heavy duty prickles. His dad watches him threateningly, waiting for him to pick up the plate.

The argument happened like this: Dianne was supposed to chop wood for the chip heater every day, so his dad could have a shower when he got home from working in the back paddock with Max, but she never did. She paid Chook to do it. He kept that a secret from his dad. He kept other secrets too, like how she and her girlfriend Bev, the store owner's daughter, used to sneak off into town all day. By the time his dad came home she'd be back, innocently cooking the dinner that Chook couldn't eat because he was too full of secrets. It was a wonder he could walk he was so heavy with them.

Sometimes Bev came over and the girls would lie on the bed and paint their nails and talk. One day, he crept in on his hands and knees without them seeing and crawled under the big bed to listen.

Dianne was saying: 'He's so jealous. I feel as if I'm in prison. Can't go anywhere, can't do nothing. I miss working.'

Bev said: 'I don't know why you stay with him, Di. Talk about cuntstruck, you must be cockstruck.'

Dianne giggled: 'Pity we can't spend all the time in bed, eh.'

Just then the fluff under the bed got up Chook's nose and he sneezed. In the awful silence that followed he tried to crawl away, but they hauled him out and shook him till his teeth rattled.

'You little perv,' Bev said. 'You wanna know our secrets, do you? Get the nail polish, Di.'

Bev held him down while Dianne got the nail polish they'd been using. It was bright blue with shiny flecks in it. Bev held out his hands, staying clear of his wildly kicking legs, while Dianne painted his nails.

'Oh, very pretty,' said Bev.

He managed to push them both away and ran into the bathroom to get the muck off. There was only cold water because nobody had chopped the wood. The nail polish just went sticky and lumpy and the smell of it made him feel like throwing up, like the stuff in spray cans. He locked the bathroom door and wouldn't come out when Dianne called him.

'Bev's gone,' she said. 'You can come out now.'

'No, you're both mean bitches.'

'Serves you right for perving.'

'Yeah, well I'll tell my dad. And I'll tell him about the wood and about you and Bev going into town.'

She panicked then and offered to pay him ten dollars if he kept quiet. That was ten times what she paid him to chop the wood.

'Get it,' he said. 'I want to see it first.'

He stayed in the bathroom till she slid a blue note under the door, then came out and let her take the blue gunk off his nails with her remover.

He ran out when she finished and put the note in the buried tin with the rest of his cash stash.

Dianne looked at him when he came back in.

'Promise you won't tell?'

Promise. They slapped hands together in a high five.

'And we're still friends?'

Of course they were. He went outside again and started chopping the wood. When he brought it back into the bathroom, she said: 'Come shopping tomorrow with Bev and me. I'll get you a coat for winter.'

It was in the army disposals store next day, exactly the coat he wanted, perfect camouflage gear. Bev reckoned it was miles too big for him, but it was the smallest they had and Dianne let him get it.

'You'll grow into it eventually,' she promised, but he hasn't so far. Nowhere near it.

CHAPTER SIX

CAMELS

As Chook finishes getting the prickles out and picks up his plate, beginning a reluctant, one-by-one, spooning of beans into his almost closed mouth, trying not to taste them before they slime down his throat, his dad offers: 'Your great great grandfather might have driven a cart like that.'

'Great great . . .?' It's too many greats.

'Yep. And wore one of them turbans like in the pictures here. He was a bit different from them blokes though, cos he was a Sikh not a Muslim. The Sikhs come from India and they're real warrior types like you and me.'

'I thought he was Koori.'

'Nah, that was his missus, I think,' says his dad.

'What was his name?' asks Chook.

'I don't know. Singh probably, like all of 'em.'

'Singh what?'

'No, something Singh.'

'What Singh?'

'I don't know, for Christ's sake. Let's call him Harry Singh. Harry the hawker. That's what he was. Keep eating.'

Chook is working round the beans, filling his spoon with sauce.

'When are we leaving, Dad?' he asks again, risking more trouble.

'I haven't decided. I already told you that. We'll lay low here for today at least. It'll take the heat off.'

'And then can we go back to . . . to the farm?'

'No way,' says Kev.

'But, Dad, I've left all my stuff.'

Tears threaten to spill out of his eyes.

'Stop sookin', for Christ's sake. Yeah, maybe we'll go back. Just to get your stuff.'

Chook already hates this place. They'd better be out of it by his eleventh birthday on April 21st. He knows it must be close because Easter is over. Max said Easter was early this year. He hid chocolate eggs for Chook all over the home paddock. The trouble was Terror found half of them before he did.

He'd like to have a birthday party on Amber's verandah like they had last year. That verandah was his all-time favourite place. It wrapped halfway round the old wooden house and it had beds and tables on it so you could sleep, eat and play there. There was a good climbing tree too that leaned up against the railing so you could climb up if you wanted to hide and talk. You were never in the way and Mrs Moran never made you go home. One time he stayed two weeks before his dad came for him. Kev knew where he was, of course.

Dianne made a cake for the party with his name spelt out on the top in silver things that looked like ball-bearings: CHOOK. His dad meant to buy him something, but he didn't get round to it. They had the party after school on a Friday afternoon. Amber's mum invited the whole school, including all six of Amber's cousins, and they had a mega pigout. There were jelly cupcakes and meringues and giant-size chocolate freckles. They played games that Amber's dad, Mr Moran, organised, like the one where you have to get dressed for a train trip in record time, piling clothes on top of other clothes, and another one where you have to stuff chocolate into your mouth till somebody rolls a six. Chook thought he was going to spew when it was his turn, it took so long! Then they played statues and musical chairs and murder in the dark. It was mad fun. There were prizes for the winners. Chook got a torch, with batteries included, that he used for playing hide and seek later that night, easily picking out the Moran boys' white faces.

Amber's dad played 'Happy Birthday' on the saxophone, then Chook blew out the candles in one big puff. Later, Amber put on CDs and the kids all danced round the verandah.

Dianne came to the party too for a while and bopped along to all the kids' music. She was seriously embarrassing. He saw some of the kids laughing at her behind their hands. When they played chasing, Dianne kept catching everyone till he told her it was time for her to go home. Chook stayed for a sleepover.

His dad wouldn't come to the party because he reckoned Amber's parents dobbed him in once for getting the dole as well as the single parent, in two different names. He had to pay back a whole heap of money. Chook didn't think it was them but Kev swore it was. He tried to ban Chook from going there after that, but Chook saw Amber and Luke every day at school and sneaked off to their house whenever his dad wasn't looking.

His dad lets him off the last few baked beans. Chook goes outside again, watching where he puts his feet this time, to rinse off the plates and spoons, as well as the empty can, under the tap. From there, he can look down the gravel driveway to the locked gate and the road beyond. Nobody walks past. He shakes the plates to dry them, taking a long look at the cart resting like an ancient animal in the shade of the date palms. It's begging to be climbed on but his dad is beckoning him from the door.

He goes back inside and Kev locks the door behind him again. He puts the plates and spoons down on the floor near his dad's bag and stows the can in a corner.

Kev is looking at the pictures on the walls. He reads out some stuff about camels to Chook. How they can eat salty plants to get water and then go for days without a drink. How they can kick in all directions, and when they don't like you, they slobber green slime all over you. Chook remembers on a camel ride on the beach up north how he had to lean backwards for the camel to get up and forwards for down. Or was it the other way round? He recalls the jolt he got as it bumped down onto its knees and how frightened he was when it yawned and showed huge yellow teeth threatening to take a piece out of him. The camel owner called out something like 'hoosh down' to get it to sit down and 'hup hup hup' to get it on its feet again. The camel kept protesting with a kind of answering howl but eventually did what its owner wanted.

The pictures show foreign men walking beside long lines of loaded camels. Chook thinks if you had a camel you'd be crazy not to ride. Or have a cart like his great great grandfather Harry the Hawker Singh.

'So,' he asks his dad, 'are we Indians then?'

'Sort of. Not really.'

'Are we Koories then?'

'Sort of. Not really.'

'But we're not whitefellas, Dad?' Chook is desperate to be something, anything, more interesting than a whitefella.

'We're a bit of everything. We're mongrels, us. We're whatever we want to be.'

'I want to be Koori,' says Chook.

'Good on you,' says his dad, patting him on the back.

Kev sits down and reaches into his pocket for tobacco. Chook crouches down beside him, watching. He's bored already. Why can't they move on? They could be on the road now, heading for somewhere, instead of stuck here waiting for nothing, eating cold baked beans, without even a toilet. His dad starts rolling another smoke, thinner even than the last one. Things are not looking good, but he'd better not say anything while his dad's got that forbidding look on his face and no coffee running through his veins.

By late afternoon, they've played four games of Uno, all of which Chook wins. He always does. It can't be good luck, since he doesn't have any, so he must be good at it. They eat a slice each out of a packet of stale white bread and have another nap in the hot, airless room with rugs. Chook hasn't dared to ask his dad again about leaving. He's still got that look on his face that says 'watch out'.

There have been no more sounds from next door. They must have gone away for the whole day. Maybe Peter has gone to school. Chook's glad he doesn't have to go. Every school except the last one sucked. It's a safe bet Broken Hill's schools suck too.

At the bush school, Mr Pike used to let him do a lot of drawing and painting, which is the only thing worth doing in a classroom. The rest of it is all 'copy this down' and 'don't talk' and 'sit still' and 'you must' and 'you have to' and all that bull. But when it comes to painting, the teacher just gives you the paint and the paper and says 'go for it'. Sweet. Chook always drew Porsches because he likes their shape, apart from them being a really good car. The only one he doesn't like is the SC because it has an ugly air dam but the rest of the 911 series is beautiful. He painted them red with a yellow and black background, so he could stick to Koori colours. He did hundreds of them in the months he was at the school. They gave him a merit award for painting, probably because Mr Pike liked those cars as much as he did.

Kev suddenly looks at his watch and says: 'Christ, it's four-thirty.'

He stands up. 'I'm going out.'

'No, Dad. Don't leave me here. I'll come too.'

'You can't come. We'll stand out like dogs' balls. I'll be quick, honest. I want to buy food and smokes and maybe some hair dye.'

'What colour?'

'Blond, baby. Like Marilyn Monroe.'

'Who?'

'Doesn't matter, forget it,' Kev says. 'I won't be long. Don't make a noise and don't go outside. I'll stop in at a pub and check the news. See if there's anything about Max.'

Max. Chook's heart thuds. Kev brushes his hair and changes his clothes. He unlocks the door and goes out into the yard, telling Chook to lock it behind him. Chook hangs in the doorway, watching, as he walks over to the fence on the units' side and looks over. Then he checks up and down the road. Chook looks too. There's nothing coming. His dad goes up and over. Chook sees him set off along the street towards town and waits till he's out of sight before he turns away and shuts the door, locking it behind him.

He hates being left alone in stray places with dead smells. His dad has done it to him often. There was that time in South Aus when he said he was going out to buy smokes and didn't come back for two days. Chook was shut in a wood shed on a mate's property, the night filled with the rustling of unknown animals and shadows flung by the moon that sneaked in the single window.

It wasn't his dad's fault, though. The car broke down on him and he had to walk into town to get a tow and then wait while they fixed it. He came home with a present for Chook to make up, the Camaro he's got now in the right-hand pocket of his trackie pants.

He carefully checks both rooms, looking behind doors and up at the ceiling, green like the walls but with a different pattern. It looks as if each square has a pineapple in it, surrounded by lollipops. He's beginning to see food everywhere. Noisy flies have buzzed in and out all day through the broken pane and now they're settling down for the evening on the ceiling. He'd better not be in this dump too long.

If he was on the farm now, he would be going out with Max on the back of the motor bike to do some last thing to the sheep. Chook didn't actually help a lot but he played round where the men were working. The motor bike could carry Terror, as well as Max and him. Terror balanced on it as if he was born to ride. He didn't take fits, so Chook patted him and threw him sticks, though Max said not to when he had work to do with the sheep.

He loved hanging round the men. When the shearers came, he and his dad worked as roustabouts, picking the wool up off the floor and heaving it onto the table. Or his dad did. They kept sending Chook outside, because one of the chicks that came with the shearers said he was in the way.

She was a slut, his dad said. Got off with all the blokes. Not his dad, though. Kev told Chook he didn't even like doing it that much; he said he got his rocks off more from riding a motor bike at maximum revs. Chook used to lie with his ear pressed against the bedroom wall when he brought women to his room. The women always made so much noise, it was hard to tell if his dad was hurting them.

When Dianne lived with them, Chook used to worry about her a lot because she called out so loud. He never heard his dad groaning or anything, though. He was quiet as a hunter. He brought that slut home one night after Dianne left and, though Chook pressed his ear to the wall, he never heard them, so they must not have done it.

It's very hot. If only he could go outside and get a drink. He wanders over to look in the glass case at Shamroze Khan's clothes. They're small, almost small enough to fit him.

The glass top lifts up easily. He reaches in and takes out the vest. He turns it over and gasps. Real gold. The back gleams even more brightly than the front. He slips it over his T-shirt. It fits him pretty well. He strokes the cool, shimmering material. It must be worth heaps. Then he takes out the baggy pants and holds them up against him. They look a good fit as well. He kicks off his shoes and puts the pants on carefully. They're old and as thin as paper. The slippers with curly toes are loose but he puts them on anyway, lifting his feet to waggle their curling tops at the walls.

He looks again at the pictures of the old camel drivers. He still needs a turban. He gets a towel out of his dad's bag and wraps it round his head. It won't seem to stay in place, bits keep hanging down, but the idea is good. Now he is Harry the Hawker Singh. Whatever a hawker is. Arra! He shouts at the pesky camels, who are bucking and rearing and kicking out in all directions.

A camel team needs a camel cart. He eyes the locked door. He shouldn't go out, but what harm can it do? His dad said not to, but his dad needn't know. He hasn't heard the neighbours come back next door. He unlocks the door and steps outside into the clear air.

The camel cart is made of mega thick timber, with enormous wooden wheels, the back ones bigger than those at the front. With the help of one of the front wheels, he climbs up and tests out the seat with his hands. It looks rotten but Harry the Hawker Singh is not very heavy and he thinks it will take his weight. Bits of rusted metal stick out, threatening to tear his thin pants. He sits down carefully, brushing away a cloud of small flies that cluster in his eyes and try to crawl up his nose.

He flicks the two front camels with his whip and rings the camel bell several times. He's got four favourite camels, he decides. Mustang, Hummer, Porsche and Ferrari.

Mustang is a big fast bull camel, very dangerous, especially when he's chasing a female. The only man he respects is Harry. 'Arra, Mustang!' Harry calls and watches Mustang bare his teeth. Ferrari is a female, very delicate and high spirited, who needs careful handling. Porsche is young, but one day he'll be as fast as Mustang. And Hummer! Good old Hummer! He isn't fast, but he's reliable and never throws temper tantrums like the others.

Harry's whipping Mustang on when he hears a voice behind him.

'Hello.'

He turns quickly. A little kid is watching him from the top of the next door fence. Peter. When did they come home? He must have been making too much noise to hear them.

'You're not supposed to be in there,' the boy says.

'Yes I am,' Chook replies, thinking fast. 'I'm Mr Harry the Hawker Singh and this is my camel cart. So piss off.'

The boy looks at him, puzzled. Chook ignores him. It won't do to show he's scared. He needs an excuse to disappear, though. Ferrari stops walking suddenly. Sore foot, by the look of things. He jumps down off the cart and goes to examine her foot, risking green slime. The little kid watches intently.

'Looks like footrot,' Chook announces. 'I'll have to get some coal tar for that.'

He seems to remember Max using that for sheep on the farm. With great dignity, aware of the boy's eyes following him, he marches off inside. As he reaches the door, the kid asks: 'Why are you wearing that towel on your head?'

Chook goes inside, snatching the towel off his head, and slams the door. He locks it and hangs the key back up on the hook, then leans against it, scared. He can't hear any talking next door. Perhaps Peter is home alone? What will he tell his mum and dad anyway? I saw Harry the Hawker Singh next door wearing a towel on his head? They'll think he's made it up. Chook takes the vest, trousers and slippers off so there's no evidence and puts them back in the glass case.

He goes into the other room and lies down on the rug, clutching his coat, trying to tell himself it will be all right. The kid doesn't know who they are. He doesn't know they're on the run. Anyway, they throw their rubbish over the fence. He'll tell the cops about that if they come round.

His stomach suddenly makes a loud, gurgling noise. He's hungry. All he's eaten all day is a few cold baked beans and a bit of stale bread. How much longer will his dad be with the food?

He listens again. At any moment there might be a knock on the door from Peter's dad. He looks up at the back window with its broken top pane. It's finally starting to get dark. His dad's been gone ages. Perhaps the cops have got him already. Chook knows what he'll do if his dad doesn't return. He'll go back to the farm and get a doctor for Max. Then he'll pick up the rest of his stuff and find Dianne. He shuts his eyes and pulls the coat over his head. If the neighbours come to the window, he'll look like some old dead soldier.

The river was shallow but Dianne knew a good deep fishing hole. They were using worms on handlines for bait. Dianne helped Chook bait the hook and throw it out deep, then they sat down to wait on a log that Chook noticed had a burnt patch. Somebody must have slept over once and their fire got away. He'd like to stay here with Dianne and light a big bonfire but he'd make sure he had a billy of water ready in case.

The sunlit edge of the water rippled past as if it was in a hurry to get somewhere, its busy gurgle punctuated by the magpies' song, like bells ringing, one just after another. Chook felt as if the sound had filled the whole of his life, along with the sad-child cry of the crow. Black on black.

'It's nice here,' Dianne said. 'Peaceful.'

There were no bites, so he soon got bored with fishing and started looking at Dianne's silver bangles that jangled when she walked, and the rings she was wearing on every finger, all silver and heavy, one in the shape of a snake with a green stone in the midst of its coils.

'Did my dad give you that one?' he asked, touching it.

'Yeah.' She glanced at it briefly. 'When he was in a good mood. Once upon a time.'

'Up north?'

She nodded. His dad hadn't been in a good mood lately, raging at both of them over nothing. Not cleaning the house, not chopping the wood, not having his dinner on the table when he walked in, not asking his permission to breathe.

'Nothing I do is right,' Dianne said. 'I dunno what he wants. He knows I love him. I don't reckon he loves me, but.'

'He does,' Chook said.

'He's got a funny way of showing it.'

Chook had to agree.

'I don't know what's the matter with him. Always flying off the handle. Maybe it's something with Max ... I know he hasn't paid him his money yet, but why does he have to take it out on us? He's got no idea how to treat a woman. He never had a family of his own, did he?'

'Yeah,' said Chook, 'me.'

'No, a mum and dad, I mean, kiddo. Brothers and sisters, that kind of family.'

'He had a dad. Once …'

'Have you ever met him?'

'Nup.'

'See? I reckon he was dragged up, not brought up, you know?'

Chook didn't know, but he nodded anyway.

'My family was pretty fucked but at least I had one. Kev told me he's been on his own since he was thirteen or fourteen. Nobody's ever given a rats about what happened to him. He took a shitload of beltings before he got big enough to fight back and put his dad in hospital. Apparently he hit him with a chair and took off.'

'He's better now you're living with us,' Chook said. It was true too.

'You reckon? I'd hate to see him when I'm not. How do you stand it?'

Chook shrugged. His dad tried his best and when he was in a bad mood, Chook kept out of his way. Dianne didn't understand that. She took him on, stood up to him. She'd never win like that.

'I won't hack it forever,' Dianne said.

Chook got up and walked away, leaving his line sitting there with a rock on it. Nothing was biting anyway. That was what he was afraid of: Dianne leaving. He started looking along the riverbank for treasures, using his Swiss army knife to dig out things. Stones, feathers, bits of iron left over from something long gone. He might even find gold. Dianne said it wouldn't look like gold, just some old rock. He smashed a couple of rocks, searching for a glint of yellow, but found nothing.

The whole day sucked. No fish, no gold. No Dianne soon. He put his hand in his pocket and felt the lucky car, the RX7, there. He held it tightly and prayed Dianne would stick around.

CHAPTER SEVEN

THE FLYING
DOCTOR

There's a smell of flowers in the air. Dianne's back. He's smiling as he opens his eyes to see a woman in the room. She's standing near him in the half dark with something over her head, like a scarf. Her skin looks black. Perhaps it's just the bad light. It's not Dianne, though, he can see that much.

Chook sits up in alarm and asks: 'Who are you?'

'I was going to ask you the same question,' she says, looking as puzzled as Chook.

She talks funny, English or something; and she smells nice, like Dianne.

She holds out her hand to him.

'My name's Khan, Dr Zarina Khan.'

Khan. That explains it. She must be a relative of the owner of this place, Shamroze Khan. Chook stands up and shakes her hand awkwardly.

'I'm Chook. We ain't staying long. Me and me dad thought your place was closed . . .'

She looks round as if searching for his dad. Chook looks too. His dad has not returned.

'It is really, but I've got a key. I come in to pray in the morning sometimes,' she says.

So she really is one of those Khans that kneel on the rugs to pray. Chook finds that very interesting. He points towards the broken window pane.

'Sorry about the glass. We had to . . .'

'I'll tell the people in charge. They'll have to get it replaced.'

As Chook looks at the window, he sees a glimmer of pinkish dawn light peeping in and realises his dad has been gone all night. The cops must have got him. The thought sends his heart racing. He hopes he didn't go round to Maryanne's place after all and bail her up, or worse still, get caught there by her boyfriend. Chook wouldn't put it past him.

He turns back towards Dr Khan and studies her, peering through the gloom of the early morning. She is tall and thin, with a long sharp nose, dark eyes and black straight hair he can see at the edge of the scarf. Over her shoulder she's carrying a bag and she does have black skin. He's sure of it. There's a shine on her face, as if she's just washed it.

'You're not Peter's mother, are you?' he asks.

'Peter, no,' she says, looking more puzzled still.

He didn't think so, because Peter doesn't have black skin, but you can't always tell.

'Who's Peter?' Dr Khan asks.

'He lives next door,' Chook says.

'I don't know anyone who lives round here.'

Chook finds that odd, since she's a Khan and comes here for praying. 'Aren't you Indian?' Chook asks.

'My family is, but we left India a long time ago.'

'So did mine. Well, one of them.'

'Really?'

She looks at him as if she doesn't believe it, because of his blond hair and hazel eyes, he supposes. All his mother's fault, the bitch. That's why you can never tell what a person is, just from looking.

'He was my great great ... something. That's his camel cart outside.'

'Is it?'

'Yeah. Have you got camels too?'

She laughs. Chook notices that her laugh is like music. It comes out as if someone is tinkling a xylophone.

'No, we live in London now. There's not a camel in sight.'

'Did you used to have some in India?'

'We actually came to London from Kenya. My grandfather was a doctor, like me, so we had no camels there either, I'm afraid.'

'My great great's name was Harry Singh, my dad told me. Harry the Hawker Singh.'

'He sounds like a Sikh.'

'How do you know?' Chook asks, amazed that she knows the same stuff as his dad.

'By the name Singh. Are you a Singh too?'

'No. I'm Chook Barlow. I never heard about this Singh until yesterday.'

'And have you still got family here?'

'Nah, they're all moved away. It's just me and my dad. We come on the bus on our way to … somewhere.' His voice trails away.

'So where's your dad now?'

'He went to get some food and he hasn't come back yet.'

Chook tries to sound casual about it, like he's in charge.

'How long has he been gone?'

'All night.'

Dr Khan looks worried.

'Where do you live? Usually.'

'On a farm. Near Sofala. But my dad's got a problem. I've got one now too. My heart's broken in two. Twice. So it's broken in four. It's got four beats.'

Chook doesn't know why he's told her that, except that she's a doctor so she should understand about hearts. Dr Khan looks at him carefully, as if she's thinking of checking it out. She'll find it's true. He counted them on the bus. It's been like that since Dianne left and now this thing with Max. Four beats where there used to be one.

Dr Khan asks: 'Is Sofala close to here?'

'Nah, it's miles away. Past Dubbo. Don't you know where it is? You gotta catch a bus.'

Dr Khan says: 'I've only been here three weeks, so I don't know lots of the places that you know.'

'Oh,' says Chook, 'but aren't you related to the owner of this place?'

'What?' she asks.

'The man that left his clothes here's got the same name as yours.'

'No,' she laughs, the same tinkly laugh, 'not at all, Khan's a very common name where I come from.'

'Why did you come here then?' Chook asks, disappointed.

'I came to Broken Hill to work for the Flying Doctor Service.'

Chook is impressed. Though he's never been to a doctor in his life, he likes the idea of them flying. They did a project at his bush school last year about Flying Doctors. He remembers something about a Reverend Flynn and that they use special words like Mike Sierra Zulu and Victor Charlie Yankee. He learnt how to spell out his name in Flying Doctor too: Charlie Hotel

Oscar Oscar Kilo. He liked the sound so much he's never forgotten how to say it. He repeats it now to Dr Khan. She looks pleased to find somebody who can speak the language.

'Zulu Alpha Romeo India November Alpha. Kilo Hotel Alpha November. That's my name spelt out,' she says.

Chook starts to spell out Amber's name as well but can't remember what B is. 'Bravo,' she tells him.

'Alpha Mike Bravo Echo Romeo,' he spells for her, pleased he can still do it more than a year later. She nods and smiles at him, as if she's thinking about something else.

Chook wishes he was a Flying Doctor. He could help people on farms who'd come off their dirt bikes and broken their legs, though not if there was too much blood or vomit involved. A clean break and a bloodless wound is how he pictures it. He imagines how grateful they'd be to him. 'Thanks, Chook,' they'd say, 'you're one in a million.' Max often called him that. One in a million. Better than the lazy shit his father calls him.

He wonders how far they can fly. Then the idea comes to him. Of course. It's perfect. Dr Khan can fly back and help Max. It'll only take her a few minutes and he could go with her, if his dad doesn't come soon. Chook has never been in a plane but he's seen those supersonic ones on TV that arrive almost before they've left and break the sound barrier while they're at it. He is so pleased with the idea he decides to ask her straight away.

'Could you fly back to Sofala to help somebody?' he asks.

'Who?'

'Max. He's lying on the bed all bloody.'

Dr Khan says: 'What? What did you say?' and takes hold of his shoulders, looking urgently at him.

'Max is hurt,' Chook says again, looking away from her intent gaze, knowing he shouldn't tell but feeling almost relieved that it's come out.

Dr Khan shakes her head as if she's having trouble understanding what he's told her and asks: 'Who is this Max?'

She's still grasping him by the shoulders and he moves slightly away so she relaxes her grip

'He's a friend of . . . mine.' He was going to say ours but that didn't sound right.

'Is there nobody there to help him?' Dr Khan asks.

'Nobody in the house? No neighbours?'

'No. We left him alone like that.'

'And how did he get all bloody?'

'My dad,' Chook pushes away sudden tears. 'Punching into him.'

That seems to make Dr Khan decide to do something. She begins looking in her bag, asking: 'Did you and your dad leave straight after he punched him?'

'Yes. And he looked real still. His chest wasn't moving. He didn't say nothing and his eyes were sort of rolled back. Dad said he was knocked out, that's all, but I don't know. He said he'd probably come to, soon.'

'But your dad didn't check on him? And he didn't get help?'

'No. We just run.'

'How long ago was this?'

'What day is it now?'

'It's Tuesday morning.'

'We must have left Saturday night because my dad always plays darts at the pub Saturday night.'

She's pulled a mobile phone out of her bag now. Chook is pleased. She'll start talking the language now. Mike Sierra Zulu to Victor Juliet Charles. Over. Instead she asks another question:

'Does Max live on his own? Wouldn't somebody have found him by now?'

'Jimmy might have come round to pick us up and found him, but I dunno. You've got a plane, haven't you?'

'I don't actually have a plane. There's a pilot who flies the team. It's not just me. There's a nurse as well.'

'You've got to hurry,' Chook says urgently.

Dr Khan nods as if she understands, but says: 'I need some details first. What's the address?'

Chook says impatiently: 'Max lives in O'Reilly's Flat. I can show you where it is, if you take me with you.'

'And that's near Sofala, is it?'

Chook nods. She's asking too many questions and not getting on with flying. He can already see the plane landing in the home paddock, scattering sheep, and he and Dr Khan running in with the stretcher to bring Max out.

'What street?'

'There's only one street. It's called O'Reilly's Road.'

'What's his full name?'

'Max O'Reilly.'

It has always puzzled Chook why Max and his farm and his street and his area all have the same name. When he asked his dad why they didn't have a farm and a street named after them, he said it was because Max had always lived in one place and was stinking rich. Chook wasn't so sure about that. Max's house wasn't any bigger than theirs and he wore old clothes from St Vincent de Paul like them. He did have a couple of farm bikes and a good ute, though.

At last, Dr Khan turns her attention to the phone and begins to press buttons. As she puts it to her ear, Chook whispers: 'Will you get the plane to stand by?' She shakes her head and holds up her hand to shush him as she begins talking:

'Hi, it's Zarina. I've got a report about someone needing medical attention near Sofala. That's not our area, is it?'

She listens for a moment. Chook is furious. She isn't even speaking Flying Doctor language and what does it matter whose area it is? With flying, one area is only five minutes away from another.

'A male: Max O'Reilly with ...' She turns to Chook. 'Head wounds?'

He nods. She repeats it.

'O'Reilly's Road in O'Reilly's Flat, near Sofala, apparently. He may already have been found, but could you put through a call to the nearest hospital and check? The police too, I guess.'

Chook shakes his head urgently. Not the police.

'OK. Thanks for that, Leanne. I'll be in at nine, so I'll see you then and get an update.'

She gets off the phone and puts it back in her bag.

'You shouldn't have told her to call the police,' Chook says.

Dr Khan looks as if she's going to say something, then she changes her mind. After a second she says: 'We work with all the services, Chook. It speeds things up.'

'My dad will kill me.'

'He'd want to make sure Max was being looked after, wouldn't he?'

Chook shakes his head. 'He's mad at him.'

'Do you know why?'

'No reason,' says Chook.

'Do you live just with your dad and Max at the farm?'

Chook nods.

'Where's your mum?'

'My mum died in a prang. Put her car into a pole, Dad said. A Valiant Charger like this.'

He fumbles in his pocket to find the car and holds it out for her to see. She moves closer to him, perhaps to get a better look at it, so he hands it to her. She studies it carefully, then gives it back to him and says: 'That's very sad. How long ago did it happen?'

'I dunno. We didn't live with her. I've been with my dad since I was two. She was the b- word. Never even changed my nappy, my dad said. And once, when we went back to see her, she promised to meet us at the station and get us a caravan, but when we got there she wasn't waiting. My dad rang her, but she hadn't got a caravan, so we got on the next train and went back where we come from. My dad said she mustn't have loved me much if she couldn't even get us a caravan.'

'Maybe she was frightened of your father?'

'That's what my girlfriend said, but I don't think so.'

'Do you go to school, Chook? Or is it holidays now?'

'I went when we lived up north, but since we've been at Max's I just stay home and help Max and Dad.'

Chook's dad told him he was getting life experience but Chook knew it was because they were lying low. If a truancy cop came round, he was supposed to tell them he had the flu. Permanently. His dad said school could wait. Kev had never gone to school himself till he was nine or ten and living with relatives. He told Chook his father had dumped him with some cousins near Melbourne for a while, when he ran off with a married woman from a sheep farm. He said the kids at the school laughed at him and called him a bushy because of the way he looked and talked, till he had to deck them. Nobody would dare to call Chook that. They were all bushies themselves at his last school anyway.

'How old are you?'

'Eleven. Nearly.'

She smiles.

'So you're ten. The same age as my nephew in London.'

'What's his name?'

'Feroz. He's a bit taller than you, I'd say. He comes up to here on me, already.' She indicates her nose. 'He lives with us, so I see him every day. I mean I used to. I miss him actually, quite a lot.'

'Haven't you got any children?'

'I'm not married, yet.' She puts her hand on his head briefly, then moves away, asking: 'Do you know why your dad didn't get a doctor for Max?'

Chook doesn't answer.

'There must have been a reason. Was he afraid?'

Chook shrugs. He's told her too much already. Now he just wants her to go and get the plane in the air.

'My dad always looks after me,' he says finally.

She looks as if she's going to say something more, then changes her mind. She fingers her bag and half undoes it.

'You know, I think you'd better come with me,' she says finally, looking very serious.

Chook shakes his head. 'My dad should be here any minute. What's the time?'

'It's quarter to six in the morning.'

'I'm not leaving my dad.'

Not yet anyway. But if his dad doesn't come back by the time it's properly light he'll get moving. Dr Khan hangs round as if she isn't sure whether to go or stay or maybe ring someone. He's got to get rid of her before his dad comes back.

'It's all right,' Chook says. 'I'll be all right. I'm worried about Max, that's all.'

He sees her reach into her bag again and find a pen and a scrap of paper.

'Here,' she says, writing, 'my mobile number. Ring me straight away if he doesn't show and I'll come back and get you.'

'He will,' Chook says, taking it and putting it in the pocket with the Swiss army knife, willing her to go, but instead she adjusts the scarf over her head and puts her bag down on the floor by the side of one of the rugs.

'I should say my prayers now. I'm running late. I usually do it at home but I've started coming here because I'm a bit homesick. They wouldn't have welcomed me in the old days when it was for men only, but now it's more of a museum . . .'

Chook knows Max's church lets women in. In fact he thinks the only people he's seen there have been women, apart from the priest. He hopes her prayers won't take as long as church seems to every week. He hears the dumty dum of the organ going on and on and the thin voices singing right down the back paddock.

He's going to be sunk if his dad finds out what he's told her. He said they weren't allowed to talk to anyone, but surely talking to a doctor wouldn't count. They're like priests, aren't they? Amber was half a Catholic and she said you could tell priests anything and they would never dob. It was the same as talking to God, she said.

Chook notices Dr Khan's feet are bare as she stands facing the upright coffin hollow. He has no idea what's going on but feels as if he should leave her alone. He shuffles into the other room, reluctantly, stuffing the Valiant Charger back in his pocket.

When he looks back at the hollow from there, it looks like a little doorway that doesn't go anywhere. She starts to whisper foreign words Chook can't catch. When she finishes one bit, she bends over and puts her hands on her knees, doing some more whispering. Then she kneels down on the rug. Chook doesn't know if Indians have the same God as Australians. He's sure they don't talk to Him the same way. He can't imagine the old ladies in hats he's seen coming out of Max's church getting down on a rug to pray like this. Or Max, for that matter. He's got bad knees.

Her voice goes on and on, the whispered words lilting. Now she's got her head on the rug. Please, let this be the last bit. Just then the door opens and Kev bursts in.

Kev was standing outside the house waiting when they came back late from the river, with the black look on his face Chook knew so well. He wanted to turn round and drive back the way they'd come. He felt Dianne tense up beside him and took her hand. His dad walked over to them and wrenched open the door.

'Where the fuck have you been?'

'Fishing.'

She got no more out before he dragged her from the car and started shaking her.

'What about the work you're supposed to do here, bitch? I get home, there's no fuckin hot water, no food, the place is a fuckin pigsty.'

'You clean it up then,' she spat at him and tried to get away.

Chook felt his stomach go into a tight knot. The wrong thing to say.

'I'll knock you cunt up in a minute, you fuckin bitch. I work all day, all you've got to do is a bit of housework. Is that so hard?'

'I'm bored stupid here,' she shouted back at him. 'I want to get away from this rotten place and get a job, have my own money again, so I'm not begging for it from you. I never wanted to come here in the first place.'

Chook could see the muscles bunched and standing out on his father's neck. He wished he could run away, fly away, be anywhere else, but he dared not leave her.

'Oh yeah, a job like you had before, glorified fuckin hooker! Christ! I give you everything, you fuckin slut, a roof over your head, food on the table, and all you do is go off looking for other blokes. You'd fuck anything in pants.'

'What? What are you talking about? I've been fishing with your son!'

'That's what you tell me!'

'Ask him then.'

Chook said: 'We did, Dad. We went fishing.'

'You keep out of it,' his dad said. He looked back into the car. 'Where are the fish then?'

'We didn't get lucky, Kev.'

'That's right, because you never went near the fuckin river. You went into town, didn't you, bitch? I got my spies. And it's not the first time. You must think I'm bloody stupid!'

Dianne said: 'No, Kev, I think you're totally fucked in the head. You take everything out on me because you're pissed off with the world and everybody in it. Face it, Kev. You're a loser.'

That did it. Before she could get her arm up, he gave her a crunching whack across the face that jolted her head back and Chook saw blood start to drip out of her nose.

He whimpered: 'Dad.'

She got away from his dad before he could hit her again and took off into the house. Chook rubbed his eyes to keep back tears. His dad looked at him then as if he saw him for the first time.

'What's the matter with you?'

Chook put his head down and tried not to breathe. He heard his dad go past him, get into the car and start it up. Chook raised his head in time to see a spurt of mud spinning from the wheels as his dad took off. As he heard the car disappear down towards town, he finally took a deep breath and tried to unknot his stomach. He stretched his body upwards and then bent in two. He did that a few times over, then walked slowly towards the house.

The front door hung half open. Chook pushed it wider and peeped in. The lounge room was empty, his little bed as sleep-tossed as ever, the TV braying out its message to nobody. He glanced sideways towards the kitchen. Empty. Then he heard sounds coming from behind the closed bedroom door on the other side of the room.

He went over and opened the door. Dianne was packing. She had hauled out her big red, white and blue striped plastic bag and was stuffing clothes into it from the open wardrobe. All the drawers of the dressing table hung open too, like hungry mouths.

He saw her T-shirt was stained with blood and her face smeared and set. She didn't look up when he came in, just kept on stuffing.

'Don't!' he cried. 'Don't go.'

'I have to, kiddo. Come with me.'

'I can't. I can't leave my dad.'

'Why not, Chook?'

'He needs me.'

She looked at him and shook her head, then turned away and went on packing. The bag was almost at the high tide mark. She pushed everything down and tested the zipper to see if it would close. It came halfway along, then stopped and wouldn't budge, no matter how she tugged. She pulled a pair of boots out of the top, tied their laces together and hung them round her neck. Then she got the bag closed.

'Will you ever come back?'

'No, but I'll call you when I can. As soon as I ...'

'What'll I tell Dad?'

'Don't tell him nothing.'

'He'll blame me.'

'No he won't. I warned him ... he knew it was coming.'

Chook slumped down on the bed. She came over and gave him a fierce hug, forgetting about the boots, which clapped him hard on the head. She rubbed it better and stroked his hair.

'I don't feel safe, kiddo. You can see that, can't you?'

He could. His dad would end up doing something worse to her. She was too stroppy for him. He snuggled against her warm breast, moving the boots aside, and they stayed like that till Bev tooted outside. She kissed him on his wet cheek and was gone.

CHAPTER EIGHT

THE ROAD TO MUTAWINTJI

Kev kicks the door shut behind him, reaches for the key, fumbles, drops it onto the floor, swears, picks it up, crams it into the lock and turns it. Then he grabs Chook and drags him down onto the floor below the front window.

'Told you to fuckin lock it,' he hisses at him. Chook is pressed against him and can feel his heart thudding. He can see cuts on his face and his hair is matted and moist. He looks as if he's been fighting. He's also come back empty-handed.

'I did,' Chook whispers. 'What's happened to you?'

Just then his dad sees Dr Khan in the next room, praying away as if she hasn't heard a thing, and his mouth drops open. He looks furiously back down at Chook as if it's his fault.

'She had a key,' Chook whispers.

'Who the fuck is she?' Kev demands, his voice hoarse.

'A Flying Doctor. She's Indian, like us,' Chook says.

'That must be her car outside. Quick, pack up your stuff.'

Chook hurries to obey. He's got to get him out of there before she finishes praying. He sees his dad throwing his gear into his bag as well.

'You haven't spoken to her? Told her nothing?'

'No,' Chook whispers. 'Nothing.'

Kev leans close to him and mouths: 'We'll take her car.'

'No, Dad!'

Dr Khan won't be able to get to the airport to save Max without her car.

'We have to get some wheels. We got no choice. We gotta get out of this fuckin shithole. Look at my head, here! They king hit me at the pub.'

Kev guides Chook's hand to a lump as big as a gobstopper at the back of his head, wincing as Chook touches it.

'Why did they do it, Dad?'

'Tell you later. Ready?'

They pick up their bags and start creeping over to the door, just as Dr Khan finishes praying. They freeze as they see her getting to her feet and putting her bag back on her shoulder. She spots his dad and comes towards them, taking off her scarf. Chook tries to get between his dad and Dr Khan, as if to shield her. She steps round him and holds out her hand to Kev, hesitating slightly when she gets a good look at him.

'You must be Chook's father,' she says. 'I'm Zarina Khan.'

He looks at her hand as if it's a funnel-web spider.

'Is that your car outside?' Kev asks.

'Yes, it is.'

She gives up on the handshake and leans down to pick up the shoes she's left by the door.

'What sort is it?' Chook asks, casually, as if they're just having a chat.

'Jap crap,' his dad says, at the same time as she says, 'Toyota Corolla.'

She looks startled at his dad's venom, then she asks: 'Why? Do you need a lift somewhere?'

'Nice try,' Kev says, 'but I'm afraid we're going to have to take it.'

'What are you talking about?' Dr Khan says. 'I'm on duty today.'

'Not any more you're not.'

'You don't understand,' she says, 'I'm a doctor.'

'Too bad,' Kev says. 'Give us the keys.'

Chook is in a panic.

'You can't, Dad!'

'Hand over the keys,' Kev says again, as if he hasn't heard him.

'No,' Dr Khan says and tries to get past him.

That makes his dad blow his top. He grabs at her bag, rips it out of her hands and starts pawing through it, looking for the keys.

'Give that back,' she demands. 'Give it to me!'

His dad finds the car keys and puts them in his pocket.

'You won't go very far,' she says. 'Chook's told me about Max.'

As soon as the words are out, Chook knows she's blown it. His stomach goes back into a knot. His father becomes very still, looking from Chook to Dr Khan.

'You told her?'

Dr Khan tries to come to his rescue.

'He just asked me to check if Max had been found. He was worried about him, naturally.'

'And he told you where he was and what had happened to him?'

Chook wants to put his hands over Dr Khan's mouth. Don't let her tell him!

'Yes, he did.'

Kev drops the bag, flies at Chook and gives him a violent slap across the head that spins him round. Dr Khan says: 'Hey, stop that!' and tries to get between them. Chook hears, without seeing, his father's fist connect with Dr Khan's head and send her to the ground.

His ear is stinging. He rubs at it and looks at his dad standing over Dr Khan, who is lying still on the floor. He's glad to see her eyes are open and not rolling back in her head.

'Did anybody know you were coming here?' Kev asks her.

'No, but they're expecting me at work. They'll come looking for me if I don't turn up. I've already made a phone call from here today,' she says weakly, touching her bruised face.

'About Max?'

'Yes, asking them to check on him. You're better off giving yourself up now and making sure Max is all right,' she says.

Chook hopes his dad isn't going to hit her again. He can see him balling and unballing his hand.

Kev says to Chook: 'Get the tape.'

Chook's hearing is fuzzy from the slap, the sound of his dad's voice echoing as if from a long way away. He goes to his dad's bag and looks in it for tape. He finds sellotape and brings that across. Kev knocks it out of his hand.

'The other fuckin tape, shithead. Gaffer tape. The brown stuff.'

Chook goes back to the bag to look for the brown stuff. He paws through it, spilling out tins of baked beans, a jar of peanut butter, some instant coffee and the plastic bag of bread. It is right at the bottom under his dad's clothes. He brings it over to him and watches him kneel across Dr Khan and spread it over her mouth, as she tosses from side to side and hits at him with her hands. The blows don't even touch him. Like a flea hitting an elephant.

When he finishes, his dad holds her hands down by her sides and says to Chook: 'There's rope in there too. Get it!'

His voice is full of rage. Chook walks over to the bag again, dreading what his dad is going to do. Tying her up is the worst thing he could do to a Flying Doctor. Chook can hear her making angry noises in her throat, and out of the corner of his eye he can see her body jerking furiously, like a puppet his dad is controlling.

Chook finds the rope they use for tying down stuff on the back of the ute. It isn't thick but it is strong. His dad rolls Dr Khan hard onto her front and ties her hands together behind her body, pushing his knee into her back. Then he winds what's left of the rope round her ankles and ties it off. He rolls her so she's on her back again, trussed up like a sheep on a spit.

Chook whispers: 'Dad, what if nobody . . .'

'Oh, they'll be here, all right! Thanks to you! It's all your fault, fuckin big mouth! They'll trace that phone call here. What else am I gunna do? We can't let her go and we can't bloody take her with us.'

Kev gets up and turns away from Dr Khan. Chook keeps his eyes down, so she doesn't see how bad he feels about his dad doing this to her. He should wear a warning round his neck: 'Beware, I bring bad luck!'

Kev picks up her bag and looks inside it again. He finds the mobile phone and turns it off before slipping it back. He pulls out a purse, opens it and counts. About a hundred dollars, Chook thinks, counting with him. He puts it back and closes the handbag.

Chook sees him put it into his bag. While he does that, Chook risks a glance at Dr Khan. She is lying quite still, watching them with big eyes. She doesn't look scared so much as amazed that this is happening to her. Chook bends down to his own bag and finds his cap that he'd packed in there to keep it away from his dad. He puts it on and pulls it low so he can't see her eyes. The smell of it is still bad. He puts on his army coat as well and makes sure that his cars and his knife are safe in the pockets of his trackie pants.

When Chook is ready, his dad goes to the window and checks outside. Then he tosses Chook the car keys and tells him to go out to the car, unlock it, put his bag in and signal if the coast is clear.

Chook turns the key in the mosque door, opens it and looks out, first right towards Peter's place, then left towards the units. No sign of anybody. He checks up and down the street. All clear. He hurries out without looking back at Dr Khan. A yellow Toyota Corolla, new-looking, stands at the open front gate. Chook sees it's got a hatchback and mag wheels. Not bad for a girl's car. He memorises the number plate. PAL 692. He opens the back and puts in his bag. He looks round once again, before waving to his dad standing ready at the door. Kev comes out and bangs the door shut without locking it.

He throws his bag in with Chook's, closes the hatchback and takes the car keys from him, getting into the driver's seat as Chook gets in the passenger side. The car starts as soon as Kev turns it on, like Max's ute did. Most cars they'd had needed a lot of encouragement or more often kicking from his dad before they agreed to start. Kev puts it into drive and they slip away from the mosque.

Chook is too scared to look at his dad. He pulls the Valiant Charger and the Porsche out of his pocket and stares at them as if he's trying to find some new feature he hasn't seen before. He fiddles with their doors. His ear still hurts, though he can hear better now. Kev looks across at him.

'Fuckin brilliant,' he says. 'Thanks heaps, shithead.'

'I only wanted to help Max,' Chook says.

'Too fuckin late. Max is dead.'

Chook knows. He's always known it but he's pushed the knowing away. Poor Max. Bad Chook.

His dad is going on: 'All I did was knock him out. He was still breathing when we left. You seen me check on him. It must have happened after.'

His voice fades as Chook sees Max again, all bloody and still, like nobody living is still. Tears come into his eyes and run down his nose. He bends over his cars. The tears fall onto the Porsche and the Valiant. He tunes in again to his father's voice.

'The cops are looking for us right now. I was going to lay low in the mosque for a couple of days but you've stuffed that up now. Good one, Chook.'

Chook can't speak.

'They put our photos on the TV news. Real old ones of us they must have found at the farm. You were about four. Remember that one with Rasta? I'm wearing a silly hat and looking like a goose. Nobody would pick us from the photos, but it would have been heaps better to stay out of sight. They'll be swarming all over the ute in Dubbo when they find it, fingerprinting and crap. Like maggots in a wound. They put the rego number on the TV, so it won't be long till it turns up.'

Chook knows it doesn't matter if they find the ute or not, now he's told Dr Khan everything.

Kev snaps his fingers in front of Chook's face.

'Hey! Talk to me!'

'What?' says Chook, from a long way away.

123

'Talk to me. How much did you tell that woman?'

'I only told her about Max needing a doctor.'

'That's all? You didn't tell her I hit him? You didn't tell her we was on the run? Bullshit, you didn't!'

Chook knows he can't say anything. They should have got a doctor straight away for Max. He didn't deserve to die. The whole thing is Chook's fault. Max loved and cuddled and looked after him whenever his dad was away. Now Max is dead. He wishes he was dead too.

'What the fuck was she doing there anyway?'

Chook says quietly: 'Just praying.'

'What?'

'Praying!' Chook shouts. Then he puts his hands over his face and cries openly. He doesn't care what his dad thinks. Gales of tears sweep through his body. He chokes and heaves with sobs, finally giving in to grief.

Kev pulls the car over to the side of the road, alarmed. He puts the handbrake on but leaves the engine running and checks in the rear vision mirror to make sure they're not being followed, before he puts his hand on Chook's head.

'Hey!' he says. 'Stop that!'

Chook tries to, but he can't. Kev hesitates, then turns the engine off and pulls Chook's head awkwardly over onto his chest, clasping it tight, knocking off his stinky cap, waiting until the crying quietens.

When Chook finally calms down, his dad says: 'You've got to understand about Max. I was only protecting you. You know that. I didn't mean to kill him. I thought he was doing bad things to you.'

Through lips soaked with tears, Chook says that he wasn't.

'Maybe you aren't the best judge of that. I thought he was. He was taking advantage. Betraying my trust. That kind of thing can warp a kid.'

Chook gradually stops shivering as his dad holds him. His mind has two bad things to sneak round now. Max and Dr Khan. Dr Khan and Max. It's too late for Max, but not Dr Khan. He wonders if Flying Doctors have any secret powers. Once at the Easter Show he saw a man with secret powers get thrown into a big tank of water, all tied up like Dr Khan. He had to escape before his breath ran out. Chook held his own breath as he watched the man struggling to get clear of the ropes. By the time the man worked himself loose and the ropes floated away, Chook would have drowned.

His dad said it wasn't secret powers but trick rope. He always told him that magic shows were a con. They once watched a TV show called 'Magicians' Secrets Revealed', which showed that magicians didn't really throw knives at their assistants. Instead, they palmed the knives, while the board the girls leaned against had knives that popped out from behind on a special signal.

Chook watched the show with his dad but it didn't make any difference. He still believes in magic. Dr Khan will need it right now.

He sits up and releases himself from his dad's hold. He runs the Porsche back and forward along his leg and moves the Valiant Charger to the other leg. Schumacher is in the Porsche and coming out of the last pit stop. There's a mechanical failure. He suddenly gets airborne and hurtles off the track, heading for the Valiant Charger that his brother Ralph is driving. They're going to crash. Boom. Next minute Michael is looking at the wreck of the car and sees his brother all smashed up with blood pouring down his face. Time for the Flying Doctor to arrive. In she zooms and in no time she's got Ralph on board and is flying away. 'We'll have him fixed up in no time,' she says.

His dad puts his hand on Chook's head and turns his face towards him.

'Now, talk to me!'

Chook pulls his head away and looks out the window. He knows his dad wants him to talk more about Max, but he isn't going to. Not now. He puts both cars in one hand and with the other picks up his cap from the floor and puts it back on his head.

'Where are we going now? To Adelaide?' he asks.

'Mutawintji, the opposite direction,' says Kev, sounding sort of relieved after all that Chook doesn't want to talk. 'We'll hang out there for a couple of days in the bush. It used to be a cattle station when I was a kid, but they've turned it into a national park now. Me and my dad used to come out here hunting pigs. The good thing is, it's always got water. Nobody will come looking for us there for a couple of days.'

His dad turns the engine back on and they start off again.

'My dad and his mates left me out here on my own once. Forgot me when they come back to the truck and I'd wandered off somewhere. I had to walk all day and half the night until I come to a property and the owner called the cops. My dad wasn't too pleased when the cops caught up with him and handed me over.'

'Didn't he want you back?'

'Nah. I was just a nuisance to him. He even tried to kill me a coupla times. Drove his truck straight at me once when I got out to open a gate. Full on. Another time he come at me with a kitchen knife. It was always worse when he was drunk. He'd go wild. He was better when he was sober but I was never special to him, you know? Not like you are to me.'

Chook knows that's true, even when his dad hits him. He's always got a good reason. He sees the wristband is twisted on his dad's arm and sets it straight. They'll be together through thick and thin, his dad always tells him. Chook won't be dragged up then dumped the way Kev was.

The dawn's pink and yellow streaks begin to fade from the sky. Kev tells Chook to look in the glove box and see if she's got anything interesting there. He finds lipstick, eyeliner, eye shadow, a bottle of hand cream and a hairbrush.

'Only makeup and stuff.'

Kev looks at the petrol gauge. Half a tank. He says that should get them the 130 ks to Mutawintji.

'She could have filled her up for us, though,' he jokes.

They drive for a while in silence through an empty landscape. Nothing moves. Then Chook remembers why his dad went out last night.

'Where's the shopping, Dad?'

'The bloody shopping. Well, that's a long story, mate. I did get some, I swear. I found a supermarket and got everything I wanted, including some blond hair dye. Then I went into the pub to have a coupla drinks and watch the news. The first thing was about Max.'

Kev looks at Chook as he says his name, but the tears are dried up for now.

'Nobody in the pub was watching. Nobody was looking at me. So I figured I could have a couple more drinks and then come back to the mosque to hide out for the night. I needed a few drinks, after all I've been through, the business with M ...' He sounds as if he's going to say Max but changes it. 'With Maryanne and that. The trouble was there was some dickhead in the bar who didn't like me talking to his missus. She just happened to be the fuckin barmaid. How was I supposed to know? Everyone chats up the bloody barmaid.'

Chook has heard stories like this too often before. His dad got into a lot of blues over women who belonged to somebody else. He never ever learnt that lesson, to keep away from what you don't own.

'I did what he asked. I stopped chatting her up. Hey, I wasn't looking for trouble, I got enough trouble. I went and sat down on me own, minding my own business, with the shopping bags still flapping round me like useless kids. I finished me last drink, got up to leave and after that I don't remember nothing. I think some of his mates must have been waiting for me outside and king hit me with a bottle or something, judging from this lump I've got on my head. It's a bloody doozy. Wonder they didn't kill me. Next thing I know I wake up on the ground in a park somewhere over near the fuckin railway station. I sit up and look for my shopping but it's gone, as well as Max's wallet. Bastards cleaned me out. I picked myself up and staggered back to the mosque and you know the rest. Total bloody stuff up all round.'

'Lucky the cops didn't pick you up, as well,' Chook says.

'Yeah,' says Kev.

'So you blew it too, Dad. Just as much as me,' Chook says, getting bolder as he sees his dad is cheering up more and more by the minute.

'Not as much,' says Kev, 'not anything like as much. I didn't go blabbing about Max for a start.'

'As far as you know. You can't remember what happened. You might have told the whole bar.'

'Maybe,' Kev says, almost cheerfully. He loves being behind the wheel of a car. It's really living to him. He floors the accelerator, speeding along the tarred road with the low shrubs and red soil a blur out the window. 'But I don't think so.'

'What'll we do about food now? I'm starving.'

'We might find something open along the road.'

The tar runs out after Stephens Creek, the first sign of life they come to. Two houses and a wide, dry creek bed with big shady trees in it. No shops there, though. Chook looks hopefully at one of the two houses because it's got an old Coke sign on it.

His dad says: 'Forget it. It's a museum now.'

According to Kev, another sign out the front says there are twelve hundred stuffed owls inside. Chook would like to see them, but Kev won't stop. He says it's too early anyway. The car rattles along the bumpy road, occasionally sliding on the drifts of soft sand that powder the rocky surface.

They turn off towards Mutawintji after forty minutes by Kev's watch. Chook works out that since they've been doing about eighty k's an hour on the dirt they must have driven around sixty kilometres without seeing another car on the flat straight road. Once he's figured that out he goes back to racing the Porsche and Valiant along his legs.

'Look,' Kev says suddenly, 'wallabies!'

Chook looks too late and misses them.

'Keep an eye out. Stop playing with them damn cars and you might see something.'

Chook puts his cars away and looks, but all he sees is a flat expanse of nothing. Kev tells him it isn't nothing. It's beautiful, he says. He points out the dark red of the soil peeping through the silvery green of shimmering bushes. Bluebush and saltbush, he calls them.

'They grow in nothing,' Kev says. 'Them and dead finish. See? That thing there. Great wood for burning. The best.'

He slows down to show Chook some prickly wattle with dead-looking branches.

'It's often the only plant with a bit of green on it at the end of a drought, but if sheep eat it, they get heaps of prickles caught in their throats. Even when the grass grows again and they try to eat, they die anyway. That's why they call it dead finish.'

Kev laughs. It doesn't sound funny to Chook, but Kev is getting more cheerful by the minute. He flicks on the radio and turns it up loud. Chook notices it's a really cool four-speaker sound system. His dad sings along, something about a mean old woman and hitting the road . . .

'That's for you, Maryanne, you bitch!' Kev says.

Chook thinks he looks really mean himself, like a hungry dingo, when he says that, with the dried blood on his face. He wouldn't like to be Maryanne, if his dad ever catches her without her cop boyfriend.

His dad had caught some disease from the dogs. Hydatids or something. He was home all day long for a couple of weeks, watching TV and bossing Chook round. Ever since Dianne left, he'd been in a foul mood. When he got home from the pub and found her gone, he went ballistic, throwing open cupboards and drawers and pulling stuff out, as if she was hiding in there. Then he made Chook put everything back.

Chook missed her too, her smell of flowers, her dancing, her laughing. He even missed her and Bev lying on the bed. He didn't miss the fights, though.

At lunchtime one day a few weeks after she left, the

phone rang. His dad picked it up and Chook saw him listening for a moment. Then he punched it down hard.

'Fuckin shitheads.'

'Who was it, Dad?'

'Dunno. They hung up. That's the second time this week that's happened.'

Chook had a feeling it might be her. She said she'd ring as soon as she got settled. He picked at his food, suddenly not hungry.

'Eat up,' his dad said. 'That's bloody good food I cooked for you.'

He'd roasted lamb shanks in the oven for hours on very low heat with some baked potatoes. Chook pulled the white flesh of the potato apart, smothered it in butter and put a little on his fork. He willed the phone to ring again, concentrating on it with all his might. When it did, he snatched it up before his dad could reach for it.

'Hello.'

'Hi, kiddo, it's me.'

He was so happy he couldn't speak. His dad asked who it was. He didn't answer, holding the phone tight against his ear as if it was part of him, bending his head, listening.

'I'm back up the coast. Got my old job back. Listen, my mobile number is 0403 629 84 —'

She didn't get any more out before his dad grabbed the phone off him and shouted: 'Don't ring again. Fuck off!'

His dad slammed the phone down. Chook tried to hide his disappointment that he hadn't got all of the number.

'Has she rung you before?'

Chook shook his head, trying to remember what he had got of it, saying it over and over to himself under his breath.

'Don't you lie to me.'

'I'm not,' Chook said.

'Fuckin cheek, trying to contact you. If it happens again, tell me.'

Chook nodded. He wouldn't, though.

His dad went muttering on about Dianne having a fuckin cheek and other worse things, like how he wasn't going to get pussywhipped by a slut like her and how she'd tried to cut his balls off, but Chook had stopped listening. He could have told his dad how she loved him. How she loved them both, but his dad wouldn't believe it. That was his problem. He never believed anyone cared about him. Still muttering and cursing, Kev turned the tap on violently and started running water into the sink to wash up, shouting at Chook to hurry up and finish eating.

At least Chook knew where to find her now. Some day, when his dad was out, he could make ten calls and work out the last digit of her mobile number. The thought cheered him up and he stuffed a big juicy piece of meat in his mouth and chewed it, trying to ignore Kev banging the plates round in the sink.

Dianne hadn't forgotten him anyway.

CHAPTER NINE

CAMPING

A little way along the White Cliffs Road, Kev sees another sign pointing to the Mutawintji National Park and takes a right turn. The road in the park is much worse, with deep, red potholes. They cross cattle grids at speed. The little car feels as if it's shaking to pieces. They stop for a flock of emus panicking across the road. Some go forward, others go back. When Kev toots the horn, they go in all directions at once. He laughs.

Chook thinks maybe things will be better out here. He'll tell his dad again how important it is to let Dr Khan go and do her job, as soon as they find somewhere to camp. Even if it's too late for Max, there'll be other people needing her.

They could ring the Flying Doctors on the mobile phone and tell them where she is. Or the pilot might ring when she doesn't arrive at work and Chook can let him know, without giving his dad up. He can speak the language after all.

They pass a turn-off to what Kev says is the old Mutawintji Gorge but he goes straight on. He isn't getting stuck down no dead-end gorge, he says. The next turn leads to the camping ground. Kev goes a little way down that road. He stops when they see two campervans and a couple of tents set wide apart on the banks of the dry creek bed. Chook spies a toilet block and wants to go in. He's dying for a real toilet with real toilet paper and real soap afterwards, but Kev says they can't risk being seen by the campers.

'Probably grey nomads,' he says. 'They drive them sort of campervans. Nosy old biddies.' Chook doesn't know what grey nomads are. They sound more like a kind of migrating bird with grey feathers than people.

He wants to ask his dad what they are but he's fascinated by where Kev is heading next. Little low walls of treated pine logs have been put up to keep cars within the camping area but Kev finds gaps big enough to steer the car through and they career over bumpy ground along the creek bank, getting well out of sight of any grey nomads. Kev follows the creek till the ground gets so rough the car stalls.

'This looks like where we're camping,' Kev says cheerfully. He gets out and walks down towards the creek. Chook stays where he is, waiting, till Kev comes back to the car.

'We're in luck,' he says. 'There's a waterhole here. Come and have a look.'

Chook gets out of the car and follows his dad down to the creek. He can't see any water in it at first, as they climb down the bank. It's steep and his dad says that's because big floods have cut into it. It all looks so dry, Chook can't imagine it in flood, but his dad says the water comes up suddenly after a few days of good rain. Right now the creek is just a whole pile of sand. Near the bank there's a greenish waterhole, which Kev says must be left over from the last time it rained.

The harsh screeching of birds in the trees that line the banks is deafening. The water in the hole looks dark and dank to Chook, but his dad says it'll be all right boiled. Kev bends down to rinse off his face and hands, pointing out the tracks of a kangaroo, its dragging tail etched in the sand. He finishes by throwing water all over his head and at Chook, who moves away, saying he doesn't need a wash. Not with that water anyway. It stinks.

'Where are we going to sleep?' Chook asks.

Kev says: 'Up there looks pretty good,' pointing at the bank. Chook looks up at the trees that shade the red dirt. Kev follows his gaze.

'Them river red gums might drop a branch on our heads but, hey, there's worse things.'

Yeah, Chook thinks. Like being on the run.

'The other tree you gotta avoid is the gidgee. They stink like a dead possum when they're wet.'

Chook doesn't know what a gidgee is. All the trees look much the same to him. Camping means one thing to Kev and another worse thing to Chook. His dad's whole life has been one big camp. Mosquitoes and sandflies don't like his blood, but they love Chook's. He comes out in big lumps from whatever is biting at the time. His dad always boils up some special leaves he knows about and bathes his skin with the lotion. It stops the bites going septic but they still take forever to go away.

Chook is afraid of the dark too, so bush nights are terrifying, with only the glowing embers to keep away wild dogs. He pictures them behind trees, waiting to pounce on him with red eyes and pointed white teeth, hungry for fresh meat. He decides he's sleeping in the car, no matter what his dad says.

He trails up to the stalled car behind his dad. Kev opens the hatchback and hands Chook their two bags. He puts them down on the creek bank about fifty metres away and sits down on top of one with his head propped up in his hands and his hat pulled low.

Kev yanks his hat off his head and throws it onto the ground, then hauls him roughly to his feet and shakes him, telling him to go and find some firewood and stop sulking.

'I can't hack sulking. I'm doing the fuckin lot here and you just sit there sulking. I got a lot on my mind now, because of you, planning where we can go next and how we're gunna get through this and what do you do? You just fuckin sulk and give me that sadsack face. I'll go off and leave you if you're not careful. I done all this for you, remember, to protect you. I spent my life protecting you.'

Chook doesn't answer. He knows it's true. His dad always has protected him. He bends down and picks his hat up, jamming it back on his head. There's wood scattered all over the ground from fallen branches. He picks up plenty and before long Kev has a fire going and a billy full of creek water bubbling away. He scrapes enough dried-out coffee from the old jar of instant to make a cup, saying there's only enough for a couple more. He and Chook toast some of the bread over the fire by skewering the slices on a pointed stick, and then smear them with peanut butter.

Chook asks his dad again what they'll do when they run out of food. Kev says they can go and see what the grey nomads have got. He reckons there might be rich pickings. He says they won't starve to death anyway.

When he finishes his toast, Chook gets out his cars and rolls them along the ground, chasing off big bull ants that instantly crawl all over them. Just his luck to be right on an ant nest. He moves his bag and his cars away and tries to brush them all off.

The smoke from the fire curls skywards. The sun is up and beaming. Birds fight near them over crumbs of toast.

'This is the life,' Kev says and lies back on the ground, then suddenly sits up again, holding his head, wincing from the pain. 'Them pricks really give me a beating.'

He dabs at the gobstopper on his head and takes another couple of big slurps of coffee, before lying back down again, on his side this time. With his eyes shut, he mutters after a while: 'I tell you what, Chook, I reckon I am a real bushy. Them kids at school was right. This feels like home.'

As far as Chook can see, his dad hasn't got an ant crawling anywhere near him. It isn't fair. He moves closer to his dad and gets his cars lined up again, trying not to disturb him.

Michael Schumacher, in the Porsche, is lapping the field in the Grand Prix. Not even his brother Ralph in the RX7 has a hope of catching him. He is into the final lap and heading for home when he clips the Camaro that Mika Hakkinen is driving and starts to spin out of control. He rolls over and over and smashes right through the barrier, hitting a man standing watching.

Schumacher gets out of the car without a scratch on him and bends over the man, who is lying still. Dead. Chook can see his face clearly, covered in blood. It's Max.

Chook rolls onto his back, away from the smash, and covers his eyes. Why is Max always getting mixed up with his cars? It keeps reminding him of the bad thing he wants to forget.

He turns his head to look at his dad, who seems to be asleep. Probably catching up after his big night.

While his dad's eyes are shut, he goes over and gets out Dr Khan's handbag. He finds the phone and turns it on. The beeps it makes wake his dad up.

'What are you doing with that?' he asks, sitting up on one elbow.

'Playing games,' Chook says. His dad watches him for a minute and sees that he's got the game Snake up, jabbing away at the buttons, sending the snake round in a constant search for targets. His dad relaxes, lying down and shutting his eyes again. Chook lets one game finish and then, keeping an eye on Kev, checks to see if the Flying Doctors are listed in the mobile's phone book. They are.

He wanders away with the phone in his hand, as if to pick up more firewood, till he's out of earshot. All he wants to do is make sure they find her. They don't have to know anything more. He'll just say: 'Charlie Hotel Oscar Oscar Kilo to Mike Sierra Zulu. Look in the old mosque! Over and out!' and leave it at that. No names, no pack drill, as his dad always says.

He presses the buttons and waits. Nothing happens. He does it again. Still nothing. There's no signal out here. He checks for messages. Nothing there either. They wouldn't be able to ring Dr Khan to find out where she is, he realises, but then he remembers that Max's mobile worked in some places and not in others on the farm. Maybe there's a chance someone will ring when he and his dad move on. He memorises the Flying Doctor number, 8080 1777, anyway.

He hopes that someone has come looking for her by now. Not the cops, though. Peter or Peter's dad, maybe. That cheers him up. After all, there will be broken people lying in paddocks, waiting for her help. His dad said the cops could trace the mobile call to the mosque but Chook doesn't know if that's true or if his dad was just saying it.

He wanders back to the fire, playing Snake again. His dad is sitting up, watching him.

'Phone work?' he asks.

'No,' says Chook. 'There's no signal.'

His father shakes his head. 'I knew there wouldn't be. Don't try and pull anything on me, Chook. I didn't come down in the last shower.'

Chook doesn't care. He feels more and more angry about his dad tying Dr Khan up. She might die there on her own, like Max did. Chook can't give up on her. He puts the phone back in the bag without speaking and realises he's still starving. He stokes up the fire, gets out another piece of bread and slips it on the end of the toasting stick. Kev asks for some too.

He finishes one and puts another piece on the end of the stick. There are only six pieces of bread left, by his count. Getting pretty stale too. Kev says he'll keep an ear out for cars leaving during the day and then they can do a reccy of the camping ground.

'Anyway,' he says, 'if we can't score anything here, we'll clear out and head for White Cliffs or somewhere with shops.'

Shops sound good. Chook crunches into the toast and pours himself some water from the rapidly cooling billy, hoping it won't kill him. Pity there's no Coke. Pity the shopping went west. He'd have liked to see his dad go blond. It'd look weird with his dark eyebrows and fierce yellowy-brown dingo eyes. He saw a combo weirder than that once in Bowraville, a guy with white hair and pink eyes. He looked like a ghost come to haunt the town. Amber said she wasn't scared. She said it was only Freddy the albino. Everybody knew him, she said. Amber could be very comforting. He wishes she was here now. She'd think of a way to get Dr Khan free.

★ ★ ★

144

The bike lurched across the shadow-fringed paddock with Chook on the back, clinging to Max's jumper. He had his arms round Max's thin waist, his fingers threading through two special holes in the wool, feeling Max's bony back press against him. Max smelt of sheep and diesel. Terror was balancing up front on Max's lap.

They pulled up near a broken bit of fence and got off. Wild-eyed sheep plunged in all directions, trying to escape and knocking into each other in a panic. Chook chased a few that hung round longer than the rest till they joined their cowardly mates.

He'd been spending more time with Max since Dianne left. She hadn't rung again, though his dad was still going on about her fuckin cheek. He could still remember her number, or at least what he'd got of it.

Max propped up the wire that the big ram had knocked down.

'Trying to get at the ladies,' Max said. They could see the old ram glowering at them from under his great curly horns at the far end of the paddock. Max told him to wait there while he went on the bike to open the gate and herd old Grumpy into the next paddock with Terror's help. Once Max got him safely bailed up in the paddock, Terror came lolloping back to Chook, while Max was shutting the gate.

Chook was searching for treasure like old bits of glass or the two cent pieces he'd found before in the grass, when Terror found a bone and started excavating for more. A thin bone, like a rib. Soon there were dozens more bones as Terror sent earth flying. Chook squatted down to get a good look at them. Some old dead sheep. More than one, by the looks of them. Chook sorted through, trying to tell what each of the bones were. There was no skull, though. He arranged some of them in a pattern, making a new creature with ribs for a nose and mouth. Dianne would have laughed herself sick at it. He missed the way she laughed like a kid. The way she jangled when she walked. The way she dyed her hair bright red and it stuck up from her head. The way she let him have a drag on her smoke and a sip of her drink.

Max was kind too, though. He'd given him some gold sovereigns to put in his secret tin and he was more into boy things, like cars, than Dianne. Dianne didn't know a Porsche from a Ferrari.

'I'll have to come back tomorrow with Kev and fix this up proper,' Max said, leaving the broken bit of the fence propped up. 'Be dark any minute now.'

He got back on the bike.

'Come on. Tea time.'

Terror flew through the air and landed in Max's lap. Chook snuggled behind him, his fingers feeling for the special holes as they chugged back across the paddock. When Max dropped him off at his house, Chook could smell the favourite tea his dad had promised him. Chicken and chips. Terror smelt it too and hopped off with him.

'Git back up here,' Max growled and Terror leapt back up on the front of the bike.

Chook headed for the door, as Max and Terror took off towards Max's house. The last thing he saw before they disappeared over the hill was Terror craning round Max to look back at him, his nose still regretting chicken and chips.

CHAPTER TEN

VISITORS

Chook is sitting on his bag, watching his father doze off again and wondering what to do next. He's got his cars lined up at his feet, but he doesn't want to play with them, for fear of killing Max again. From time to time he hears the sound of a car on the road not far away and gets hopeful that maybe someone will come snooping round and force his dad to move on, but the car always goes away.

The sun is hot and getting higher in the sky. He pulls his hat low over his eyes. His dad must feel the sun on his face, because he wakes suddenly and sits up, yawning and rubbing at his sore head. Noisy brown and black birds come close to them, pecking at crumbs almost under their feet. They fight over scraps like vicious dogs, then, next minute, they turn round and start grooming each other.

'Apostle birds, that's what they're called,' Kev says, watching.

'What?' Chook says.

'Apostle birds, because they're always in groups of twelve. Count 'em.'

Chook counts. There are exactly twelve.

'See? Like the apostles.'

'Who are they?'

'The followers of Jesus. The first ones. They was called apostles.'

Chook is surprised how much he's finding out about religions. He's also surprised birds can count up to twelve. He wades in amongst them, trying to scare them off, but they don't scare easy. They're as tame as kittens.

'People also call them happy families,' his dad says.

'Happy families?' Chook says. 'But they're not!'

'That's why they call them that. They're about as happy as the Barlow mob.'

'But . . .'

Chook wants to ask why they are called something they're not, but his dad cuts him off, standing up and stretching.

'How about a walk?' he says.

'Where?' says Chook, dully.

'Along the creek. Thatta way.'

He points in the opposite direction from the camping ground. As Chook hesitates, his dad punches him playfully on the shoulder and says: 'Come on. Lazy shit. It'll do you good.'

His dad sets off, skidding down the bank. Chook trails after him along the creek. His dad's nap seems to have livened him up. He points out all the tracks he sees in the sandy bed and tells Chook what animal made them. Chook listens with half an ear, then wanders off on his own. He takes out his knife and whittles away at a bit of stick. He whittles so much it snaps in two and he throws it away.

He has a look round for crystals. You can find perfect ones if you know where to look. Near creeks like this is often good. His dad found a whole heap of them up a bush track near Taylor's Arm. He and Huey were growing dope off the track and they were up there checking on the plants when Kev came upon the crystals. He hid some by the track for later, traded some in the pub for parts he needed for his car, but he and Chook kept some for themselves. Chook wonders where they are now. Back at the farm, most likely.

There's a lot of special energy round crystals. When his dad showed them to him up the Arm he could hear a loud roaring noise and he asked his dad if there was a plane somewhere. His dad got worried because of the spotter planes the cops send over to check on dope, but it wasn't a plane. It was only the energy of the crystals making the sound.

Huey or somebody must have blabbed about where the crystals were, because next time they went back, the crystals had all gone and also the dope plants, just ready for harvesting. His dad was ready to kill somebody that day, if he could have found out who did it. Chook told him not to worry. The crystals would bring them bad luck for sure. He feels his stomach go tight, thinking about how Huey copped it only a few weeks later.

He can't see anything that looks like a crystal. No sounds, no energy either. He picks up a river stone, running his fingers over its smoothness, enjoying the way it traps the heat. He crouches down, holding it to his ear.

His dad has walked on ahead, but comes back when he sees Chook has stopped.

'What are you doing?'

'Listening,' Chook says.

'To what?'

'To the stone breathing.'

'Stones don't breathe,' his dad says.

'Yes they do,' Chook says. 'But they don't breathe like us. They breathe through moss or dirt.'

'Is that so?' Kev says.

It is, Chook is sure. He believes that everything has life, even stones, so they must be able to breathe. You can't see them breathing, of course, they do it secretly.

You have to listen very hard. Kev shakes his head and walks over to stand near the waterhole.

'It looks pretty deep near the middle,' he says, chucking pebbles in to test.

Next minute, he pulls off his jeans and T-shirt and starts wading naked into the water. Chook watches him from a safe distance.

'Come on, you could do with a wash,' he calls, as he gets in deeper. It only comes up to his waist in the middle but he ducks under so his shoulders are covered and throws water over his head. Chook doesn't want to join him. The water is dirty. There might be bullrouts in there. That's a kind of mean-looking spiky fish you get in weedy creeks up the Arms. They lie in wait on the bottom and if you tread on one with bare feet, watch out! A bullrout's sting nearly put him in hospital once, it was that bad. He can still remember the pain doubling him up till his dad got worried. Kev put some blue stuff he kept specially for stings on it and said if it didn't get better in an hour or two he'd drive him into town for treatment. He didn't need to. The blue stuff worked.

There's one pickled in a jar in the Bowraville Museum but, when his school visited, Chook only took one peep and then had to look away. It was ugly enough to give him a pain all over again, with its flat head, white eyes, vicious whiskers and spikes and

152

brownish-yellow sort of colours. That waterhole looks like a definite bullrout hangout.

He stays sitting where he is, holding the breathing stone. Next minute his dad comes streaking out of the water, picks him up and runs back with him screaming into the waterhole, fully dressed. Chook beats at his dad and drops the stone but he can't escape. His dad pushes him right under the water and holds him there till Chook thinks he will drown. He comes up, spluttering and furious, and jumps on his dad, punching at him. Kev is laughing the whole time. He's like a big kid when he's in a good mood.

Chook tries to wade out, hating the squelchy mud and the tree roots under his feet, thinking at any moment he'll feel a sting, but his dad hauls him back in. Chook can't swim very well and, ever since his bullrout experience, only likes shallow swimming pools with clear blue water so he can see what he's up against.

'There's no escape, buddy! You're staying in with me,' his dad says.

Chook wishes his dad wasn't so cruel and took more notice of what he was afraid of. Kev always tells him he's got to be cruel to be kind, because he hates weak people and wants to make sure Chook is strong. He always tells him: 'Only the strong survive.'

Chook eyes his dad's powerful chest with its smudges of old blue tattoos and thinks, without wanting to, of

Max. He imagines he can still see a splash of Max's blood on his dad's neck, near his ear. He pushes his dad away and bobs up and down with his eyes shut, trying not to think of anything. Not what might be under the water. Not what happened on the farm. Not what happened with the Flying Doctor. Not what might happen tomorrow.

They hear cars passing occasionally on the road about five hundred metres away and listen each time, but Kev says that nobody would ever know they were there, not even stickybeaks like grey nomads. He says they're too far away to hear them and won't come walking so far along the creek. They'd be too old for long walks, he says.

They stay in the water till Chook says something is definitely biting his toe. When his dad asks him to show him, he holds his foot up above the water, but there's nothing there. His dad finally takes pity on him and piggybacks him out, holding him high on his shoulders with strong arms. He throws him down on the soft sand of the bank and then pins him down. Chook fights back and they have a good rumble in the sun.

The wind has got up and they think at first the sound of the vehicle approaching is the wind rushing through the river gums with a roaring sound.

By the time Kev realises someone is coming, the vehicle is close. He pulls Chook to his feet and starts running. Chook sprints after him across the creek. They hide in a little thicket of trees, crouching low and breathing heavily. Chook goes to ask his dad a question.

'Shh,' says Kev, pointing to a car, which is lurching along like a ship wallowing in big seas, very close to their campsite.

A powerful white four wheel drive stops beside the Corolla. Chook can see three heads inside. They sit there for what seems an age, looking round.

'Come on, come on,' Kev mutters. 'Get it over with.'

'Is it the cops?' Chook asks.

'Shh!' Kev says again.

Finally the driver opens his door and gets out slowly. He is middle aged, Koori, with a beer gut, wearing a khaki uniform. Another Koori man gets out the passenger side, also in a khaki uniform. The two men stand looking at the Corolla. Chook can't hear what they are saying. Jap crap, probably. Then they walk over and look at the fireplace and his and his dad's gear.

From the inside of their vehicle, the third man, an old Koori, looks out directly to where Kev and Chook are hiding. It's as if he can see them. Or smell them. Chook knows that old Koori people definitely have secret powers. The two others look back at the old man and he gives a slight nod towards where Chook and his dad are hiding.

The men saunter down to the creek bed. Kev and Chook's helter-skelter tracks must be clearly visible heading across the creek and into the little thicket. As the men approach them, Chook clutches at his dad, but Kev pushes his hands away.

'It'll be all right,' he says.

When the men are almost on top of them, he steps out. Chook sees them grin at his nakedness.

'Gidday,' says Kev. 'Sorry I'm not dressed. I wasn't expecting you.'

The two men grin even more broadly and extend their hands. Kev shakes them one after another.

'No worries,' the one who was the driver says. 'Get dressed and we'll have a yarn.'

At this point Chook creeps out from the bushes in his wet clothes.

'This is my son,' Kev says.

'Gidday,' the men say.

Chook holds out his hand and introduces himself.

'I'm Chook.'

'Gidday, Chook,' they say again, shaking hands with him too.

Kev and Chook lead the way back across the creek to their campsite. The men wait quietly, sitting themselves down by the dead fire, as his dad gets dressed. Chook decides he'll let his clothes dry on him. It's so hot it won't take long.

The old man gets out of the car and joins them. He is very dark and thin as a stalk, with eyes so black they disappear into his face. Even the whites of them look muddy, so Chook only catches a glimpse of them when they glitter. As Kev and Chook take their places round the fire, the driver introduces them all.

'I'm Reg and this is my cousin Lyall. We're the rangers. And this is our uncle, Cliff McKenzie. He's the elder round here.'

There are nods all round and Chook hears his dad say his name is Geoff. Geoff! Where did that come from? His dad starts to revive the fire and tells Chook to get some more firewood.

Reg, who seems to do most of the talking, says: 'Hang on a mo. That's the reason we're here, see. We saw the smoke from your fire this morning. Trouble is, there's a complete fire ban outside designated areas. And this ain't a designated area.'

Chook hears his father say: 'Sorry, bro. We didn't realise ... The thing is, we have to cook.'

Chook can hear the relief in his dad's voice. They're rangers, not cops, and all they're worried about is bushfires. They don't know anything about Dr Khan or Max. Chook hopes he'll get a chance to take them aside before they leave and tell them about Dr Khan, without his dad knowing.

Reg, who seems to do all the talking, asks: 'No gas, man?'

'No gas,' Kev answers. After a pause, he goes on: 'Look, bro, I've been lighting fires all my life and never had one get away.'

Reg says: 'Yeah, but that's not the problem, see.'

'I remember coming out here hunting with my dad when I was a kid. We lit fires and camped wherever we liked.'

'You lived out this way?' Reg asks.

'Broken Hill,' Kev says.

Lyall speaks for the first time: 'Times have changed, bro. Mutawintji was a cattle station in them days.'

'That's right,' Kev agrees.

'Well, now it's a national park, see. No shooting, no dogs, and no fires or camping except in designated areas. That's the new rules.'

'It's tough, man,' says Kev, 'when you're not used to it and you got no gas.'

There is a long pause. Chook can see that, though they have to stick to the rules, they understand what his dad is on about. Like his teacher, Mr Pike, at the last school, who always seemed to understand where he was coming from, even when he had a blue with Amber's cousin, Tait Moran. Tait shouldn't have laughed at his runners, just because they had holes in them. Chook gave him the usual warnings, following his dad's rules: two 'get out of my face's'. But Tait wouldn't stop taking the piss, so he had to hit him. Mr Pike did keep him in at lunchtime but the two of them had a ball, playing cards and talking.

Reg says: 'Yeah, I know, bro, but the good thing is now we own the place. In them days, we just worked on the station for the white fellas. Now it's ours and we can look after our sacred sites properly.'

'No shit. Good on yers,' Kev says.

'Yeah, we had a bloody big hassle to get it. We closed the road in the eighties, blockaded the place, because we could see the damage people was doing; anyhow, finally the government backed down and give it to us.'

Kev says: 'That's great, only I thought that now you fellas run it, camping and hunting and that should be allowed . . . for Koories, at least, eh?'

'No,' says Reg. 'We run it with the National Parks and they're into conservation, man, not hunting.'

'I'm into conservation too, yeah, I'm a real greenie,' his dad says, 'but fires are part of the natural cycle, aint they?'

They nod and shrug. Reg says, pointing: 'If you was in the camping ground along there, you could light as many fires as you like.'

'Yeah, mate, I know,' says Kev, 'but I hate camping round other people. Feels like I'm in the suburbs.

I want to do me own thing, you know, wake up and see the birds, not somebody's fuckin washing.'

There is another silence before Reg speaks again: 'You boys here for long?'

'Dunno,' says Kev. 'Could be a while. I want Chook here to have some of the experiences I had when I was a kid. He's missed out on a lot.'

Chook doesn't want to put a spoke in his dad's wheel but he'd like to tell them he could do without a lot of the experiences his dad is talking about. He'd rather be back on the farm now, collecting his stuff and double checking on Max, because he's been thinking about it and he isn't sure that Max is dead.

Maybe he's in a coma like that mate of his dad's in Bowraville who came off his motor bike and spent six months in hospital, like a vegetable, then suddenly came round. Just woke up. That could happen to Max. How bad would it be to bury him when he's still alive? The thought makes Chook shiver. Amber has told him stories about people being buried alive. They find scratch marks on the undersides of their coffin lids. He has to get back to the farm and make sure that doesn't happen to Max.

Finally Reg comes up with something: 'We could probably give you a lend of some gas and a stove.'

'Tops,' says Kev, 'though I'll miss my big fire to go to sleep by. I love lighting a log, bro.'

They all nod. Chook can see the Koories think it's a bummer, too, but the new law is the new law and they've got to stick to it.

'Tell you what,' Kev says. 'How about a brew before you go? It'll be a long wait for one otherwise. Give us one more fire, eh, bro?'

There is a pause and then Reg says:

'Yeah, just the one.'

Within minutes, Kev has the billy boiling again. He scrapes hard on the coffee jar but three cups is all it offers.

'That's all right,' he says, 'you blokes have it. I drink too much of the stuff.'

Chook hates the thought of what he'll be like if they don't get more coffee soon. And more smokes. He's down to using the butt bag, Chook sees. Reg sees it too and offers him a tailor. The old man rolls his own. White Ox. Chook gazes up at Reg and tells him he's a Koori too. Sort of.

'Course you are,' says Reg. 'Only you was born in the middle of the day and got that fair skin and them blue eyes and I was born in the middle of the night and got my black skin and brown eyes.'

Chook is delighted that Reg can tell he's one of them. He puts up his hand and Reg gives him a high five. He looks over at Lyall who smiles at him too.

Kev laughs. 'Yeah, trouble is we haven't spent enough time out here with you people learning some of the law and the old stories. Chook's missed out real bad. And me too. My old man never settled anywhere. Jack of all trades and master of none. Dragged me all over the countryside so I never felt part of nothing.'

'You want to stay out here for a bit,' Reg says. 'We got a Heritage Centre and elders like Uncle Cliff here tell us the old stories. We bring out kids from the towns to listen and learn. You want to stick round. We got a tour this arvo. Just starting up again after the summer break. We'll take you out bush to see some peckings and hand prints. You'd like that, eh, Chook?'

Chook nods, though he doesn't know what peckings are.

'Do you know how the waratah turned red?' he asks.

'Maybe, but we mostly tell the stories from round here, handed down through the age. Uncle Cliff here has got hundreds of stories.'

Chook looks expectantly at the old man, who sucks contentedly on his mug of coffee but does not speak. Chook whispers to Reg: 'Can your uncle talk?'

'Yep,' says Reg. 'He just don't choose to very often.'

Just then Cliff is doubled over with a coughing fit that sounds like it'll never end. Every time Chook thinks it's over, another choking wheeze comes.

'It's that White Ox cough,' Lyall says. 'It's gunna kill him.'

'Tell you what I could do with, Reg,' Kev says, as Cliff's coughing finally quietens, 'finding some pituri. You know where there's some round here?'

Chook doesn't know what pituri is but he knows his dad will be hanging out for some weed. Maybe pituri is a Koori name for it. Kev smokes weed whenever he can, which is most days.

Reg says that his uncle might know where there is some. Cliff gives them a sly, weak grin, still recovering from the coughing fit, but says nothing.

They finish their brew and their smoke and get to their feet.

'We'll bring the gas later on today, Geoff. After the tour. And if you want to go on it, it starts from the camping ground. Two o'clock.'

'No worries. Thanks, bro,' says Kev. 'And I'd appreciate it if you kept quiet about us being here. It's a secret from the missus. She don't appreciate the boy getting out into the bush. Wants to make a baby of him. You know?'

The men laugh as if babying by the missus is a well-known problem. They get back into their four wheel drive, and make their way back along the rough ground towards the campsite and the road. When they hit the road Chook and Kev hear them turn left and then, after a while, left again.

'Must be a ranger station over the back there,' Kev says. 'They got it pretty well hidden.'

'What was that about me being a baby?' Chook asks, as aggressively as he dares.

'Bullshit, that's all, mate. I had to think of some excuse to keep 'em quiet about us being here. That's the first thing I come up with.'

'And your name isn't Geoff either!' says Chook, still indignant.

'I thought it suited me,' says Kev, lightly brushing his hand over Chook's head.

'Nothing suits you, Dad. Except Trouble,' says Chook, jerking his head away.

Kev laughs. 'That's not my fault. Trouble sticks to me like shit to a blanket.'

'And what's that stuff you want them to get for you?' Chook asks.

'It's a plant that Koori people chew. Gives them a bit of a buzz. Not such a big bang as dope, but it'd help.'

'Can we go on the tour with Reg?'

'Don't be stupid,' Kev says. 'Are you kidding? We're on the run. We can't go showing up in front of a whole pile of tourists and bloody school kids.'

Though Chook knows it's true, he's disappointed.

'Tell you what, though,' Kev goes on, 'it gives me an idea. The camping ground along there will be empty, if they all go on the tour. Perfect time to check it out for munchies.'

Chook knows they've got to do something about food a.s.a.p. He's hungry again right now. His dad gets out another tin of baked beans when he tells him he's starving. At least these will be hot, Chook thinks. Kev opens the can and slops them into the billy.

'Nice of them to ask you,' he says. 'Good blokes. I thought it was the pigs at first. What a fuckin relief. Koories would never give you up. Here.'

He hands Chook a piece of bread to toast and gets another one out for himself while the beans splutter into life in the billy. Only four bits of bread left.

'We won't be able to have toast like this once the fire goes out. Bloody stupid, this fire crap. All because of city slickers who don't know what they're doing. I've never had a fire get away from me in me life. I know what I'm doing in the bush, that's why. Those blokes were on my side, I could see that. But they've got to do what the bloody National Parks tells them to do.'

Chook listens to this absentmindedly. He's remembering toasting marshmallows with Max. When there was just the two of them, Max would sit him on his lap in front of the open fire and they would toast them together, then pop them into their mouths, feeling them melt into a delicious, slightly burnt pile of sugar. He slaps at the flies swarming round his face and burrowing into his nose and eyes.

He didn't get a chance to tell the rangers about Dr Khan. Maybe later when they come back with the gas he'll manage it. And what about Max being buried alive?

'Dad,' he says, 'you know Lance, how he was a vegetable, but then he woke up?'

'He was in a coma, yeah. What about it?'

'Do you think that could happen to . . . to . . . Max?'

His dad looks at him quickly. He is spooning hot beans onto toast.

'It could, but . . .'

'They wouldn't bury him alive, would they?'

'Nah. They'd get a doctor to check that he was really . . . you know . . .'

His dad doesn't finish the sentence. He hands Chook a plate and starts eating. Chook looks at his plate. Doctors have made mistakes before and his dad knows it.

'That was why . . .' Chook begins. 'I wanted to get Dr Khan to go back and check on him. Just in case . . .'

'Yeah, yeah, yeah!' his dad cuts him off. 'Don't you worry about it. Eat up and shut up.'

Chook bends stubbornly over the plate of baked beans. He'll worry about it if he wants to. His dad can't stop him.

166

★ ★ ★

Chook was playing cards with his dad and Max. They'd finished several hands of five hundred when he suggested teaching them spit, a game Amber had shown him at school. It was wild, a two-handed game of patience combined with snap, so the winner wasn't the one who went out first but the one who snapped the smallest pile of remaining cards first. It was a slaughter whenever he and Amber played.

His dad learnt pretty fast but Max was hopeless. Maybe at fifty-three he was too old. His dad was only forty-three. Max's reflexes were as slow as his brain. He'd be blinking and scratching his stubbly face while Chook shouted 'five on the six, Max', or 'queen on the king'. And Chook would wait to snap when he was finished, holding off, holding off, till all the fun went out of it for him, though his dad thought it was hilarious. He kept on winning and Max kept on saying 'oh gawd!' and his dad kept on laughing. 'Seven on the eight, Max!' 'Oh gawd!'

'You're too flaming fast for me, Chook,' he said.

'It's the quick and the dead, Max,' his dad said.

'Well,' said Max, 'I must be the dead.'

Max gave up in the end and went to put a big lump of ironbark on the dying fire. As the flames picked up and started whooshing up the chimney, Max brought out some marshmallows, like he did whenever Chook came over. It was Chook's job to toast them on the end of the fork, though he got into trouble from his dad for eating twice as many as the other two. He'd count wrong: 'one for me, one for you, one for me, one for me, one for you ...'

Eventually his dad picked him up, all sticky with marshmallows, and held him over his shoulder saying: 'Bedtime, mate.'

'No, no,' said Chook kicking at him. It wasn't fair. Just because he couldn't stop yawning didn't mean he was tired.

'Let him stay up a shade longer,' Max said.

'Nah,' said his dad, 'look! His eyes won't stay open.'

His dad held his hand over Chook's eyes, keeping them shut, though Chook pulled at his dad's big paw as hard as he could.

His dad carried him to the bedroom and put him into his double bed.

'Night, boyo,' he said, in his funny voice. He called it his Welsh accent. It usually meant he was in a good mood, though not always. He gave him a big, smacking kiss on the top of his head, which meant he was in an extra good mood. He went to go and turn out the light. Chook made a move as if to get up but his dad held up his fist in mock threat and Chook giggled and snuggled down in the saggy bed.

He heard Max offer his dad a smoke when he went back to the lounge, then he heard the cap coming off a new bottle of beer and the slap of cards being dealt on the table. He strained to hear if they were playing spit. No, he could hear the clink of money on the table. Poker. A much quieter game.

He drifted off to sleep to the sound of their talking, trying to make out what they were saying. Max's voice was deep and growly and hard to understand, and his dad's was tough and sinewy. He heard them laughing. It'd be good if his dad and Max got on well enough for them to be able to stay a while. He was just starting to feel settled and cosy on the farm, even without Dianne. It was beginning to feel like home.

CHAPTER ELEVEN

FOOD

Chook can't finish the plate of beans, even though he's starving. They taste bad.

His throat feels as if it's got something caught in it, like a sheep choking on dead finish. His stomach is hurting again too, angry about the treatment it's getting. He lifts up his T-shirt and looks at his ribs. The skin is so thin over them, it looks as if the bones might break through at any moment. He's always been able to count his ribs by feeling them, Max often teased him about it, but now he can see them all clearly as well.

His dad doesn't seem to have any trouble swallowing the beans, so Chook doesn't dare say they're off. In fact, his dad finishes Chook's beans as well. Chook tries to remember what he has eaten since Saturday night. Apart from the Sausage and Egg McMuffin that he only picked at, and the hamburger and chips on Sunday, he's survived on slimy beans, bread, peanut butter and stinky creek water. No wonder he feels funny in the head. His ear still hurts too, from where his dad whacked him.

He can't stop thinking about food. Dreaming about it. Remembering his favourite munchies. Mrs Moran's cooking. The best part about Amber's mum was that she loved cooking food for kids. The more people there were to cook for, the happier she was. She used to make pancakes with cream and jam for breakfast when Chook stayed over. One lunchtime she made twelve tomato and cheese toasted sandwiches for Amber and Chook and Amber's brother Luke. They just kept on coming.

Amber said it was because her mum wasn't an Aussie. She was from one of those countries where they like to eat. Chook often thought he'd like to stay there forever, just sitting in the kitchen sniffing the air.

From his feet to the top of his head he's feeling sorry for himself, when he hears the rangers' four wheel drive coming back along the road and turning into the camping ground. Kev is instantly alert.

'That's them,' he says.

'Are they bringing us the gas?' Chook asks.

'No,' his dad says, 'it'll be the tour. With a bit of luck the camping ground will be empty soon. Let's go.'

Chook scrambles to his feet and starts off, but his dad reminds him they'll need something to carry any food they find in. He gets Chook to tip the clothes out of his bag, since it has the least in it, and then they set off, Chook stuffing his cars in his pockets for luck and pulling on his cap.

It's uneven walking along the creek bed and Chook stumbles along behind his dad, kicking at the hot sand. He sees a black snake sunbaking near a log and gives it his special snake look that says 'brother'. The snake doesn't move. Flies crust on his dad's back. Chook swipes at them, trying to catch one and his dad turns round and gives him a threatening look.

'Flies,' Chook explains.

The camping ground is a few minutes' walk away on a bend of the creek. They hear vehicles moving round before they see them.

'That'll be the campers getting ready,' Kev says.

When they spy the first tent, the two of them get down low so they can just peep over the high bank. Immediately Chook feels an army of bull ants swarming up his legs. With his usual luck, he's landed right in the middle of a nest again. He shifts and tries to brush them off, feeling his father's hand on his arm, warning him to be quiet.

In front of them is a brownish-coloured tent with clothes hanging out to dry on one of its ropes. Kev points it out, whispering: 'See what I mean about the fuckin washing?'

A fold-out table and chairs sit in front of it, with a huge blue esky under the table. Chook's mouth waters as he looks at the esky. That's what they're after. To the right of that tent there is another smaller tent, green and shaped like a dome, which is zipped up and looks deserted, like the first one. Further along the bank there are two campervans which also look closed up.

Beyond the line of campsites, all twelve apostle birds are having a noisy, quarrelsome swim in a puddle under the tap. Over near the toilet block at the back, they can see Reg and Cliff standing by their four wheel drive, talking to about eight campers. Chook wonders if they're grey nomads. The rangers are leaning against their car, as if they have all the time in the world.

'I wonder where Lyall is,' Kev whispers.

There are three vehicles lined up behind the rangers'. Two are four wheel drives but the third is a cool Camry.

Chook is sorry that he can't go on the tour with them. The rangers belong to him, not them. They're his people. He feels like showing himself to them, calling out or waving, just so they know he's there.

Suddenly a bus full of school kids swings in to view and pulls up near the rangers.

'They must have been waiting for the kids to arrive,' Kev whispers to Chook.

Chook looks at the bus full of kids, their heads silhouetted in the windows, and feels as if they are another species, from Mars or Jupiter. Like the aliens he saw in the flying saucer that time. Or maybe he's the alien. He hasn't played with any kids for nearly a year, not since he's been at the farm. Dianne and Max were both like big kids, so he didn't really miss any of them, except Amber.

They see Reg go over and speak to the bus driver, pointing up the road. The kids are bouncing up and down in the bus, Chook observes sourly. No respect.

Then they see Reg go back to his car and he and Cliff get in. The campers hurry into their vehicles and they all take off, with the rangers setting the pace in the lead and the rest trying to keep up. The convoy goes out of sight, though Kev and Chook can hear them grinding up the rocky road for a while afterwards.

Kev and Chook look hungrily at the tents and campervans and especially at that blue esky. Kev stops Chook heading straight for it.

'It might all look empty,' Kev says, 'but there could be people asleep or anything. Follow me.'

They climb up the bank using some tree roots that stick out like a giant's frozen fingers and Chook follows Kev round all the campsites.

'Hello! Hello!' he calls, outside each of them. There is no answer.

'What would you say if there was?' Chook asks him.

'I dunno. Probably, is Fred there?' Kev says.

'Who's Fred?' Chook asks.

'A good name for a grey nomad, you goose.'

'What's a grey nomad?' Chook has to ask finally, telling himself he is not a goose. Geese are fat and well fed.

'Old people who take off and travel round Australia when their kids are all grown up. They've paid off their mortgage or whatever they've got and they say hooroo to the suburbs and turn into gypsies like us.'

Chook thinks that when he's old he'd rather have a farm named after him and stay put on it.

'What if there really was someone called Fred?'

'Then I'd make up some crap or other.'

Kev sounds sick of his questions. Not enough coffee or smokes, Chook thinks gloomily. They'd better find some soon or he's in deep shit.

The people have all gone. The camping ground is theirs for the taking. They go back to the first tent with the blue esky. Everything is neat and tidy, from the washing hung by colour, to the shoes lined up in pairs at the doorway of the zipped-up tent. Kev bends down and pulls the esky out from under the table.

'Heavy as buggery,' he says, as he lifts it onto the table. Good, thinks Chook, it'll be loaded with food.

Kev opens it and says to Chook: 'Whoa! Will you look at this!'

Chook looks in. It's brimming with food. Fairly swimming with it. His saliva glands go into overdrive. Chocolate biscuits. Coke. Cheese. Cold meat. Eggs. Bread. His mouth waters and his hands reach out, but Kev says they shouldn't take so much that the people miss it straight away.

When Chook begs for a biscuit to stop the hunger pains, Kev gives in. He probably wants one just as much. They open the packet and take out three each, then put the rest in their bag. Chook bites into the first one. It's got mint inside, like a soft cushion, and the outside melts in his mouth. He could eat a lot more than three. He could eat the whole packet, but his dad stops him, saying they have to sort out what else they should take.

It doesn't take them long to decide, and in the end, they take only one bottle of Coke, some cheese, a packet of bacon and half a dozen eggs.

'We can come back another day,' Kev says, 'and we've still got these others to check out.'

They arrange the rest of the stuff carefully to cover the losses and put the lid back on. Kev lifts the esky back down under the table.

'Feels a bit lighter,' he says, as, giggling like school children at a midnight feast, they dance over to the second tent, with their precious haul in Chook's bag.

This tent's a small, two-person job. Chook feels awkward as they go in, looking at the double sleeping bag resting on a velvet blow-up mattress. It's like walking into someone's bedroom.

There's no food in sight, just the bed with two neat pillows and a book on either side of them. Kev looks at the books, tempted to take them, but once he reads the titles he changes his mind. He says they look too heavy, like literature. Kev reads books with the corners all turned over. He calls them his who dunnits. There's usually a woman on the cover with blood on her white dress.

'Maybe they keep the food in their car because of ants,' Kev says.

'Haven't they ever heard of eskies?' Chook asks in disgust. He wants to leave, but sees Kev tramping over the bed and looking under each of the pillows.

Chook says: 'Dad, don't!'

'Jackpot!' Kev calls. He holds up a bag of weed and some condoms.

Chook says: 'Yuck, that's disgusting,' when he sees them.

'I had a feeling ...' Kev says. 'Musta smelt it. Fuckin love nest, eh.'

He opens the bag of weed and has a good close-up sniff of it.

'Smells beautiful,' he says.

'But we can't eat it,' Chook says.

'There's more to life than eating.'

Not right now there isn't, Chook thinks. Kev puts the weed in their bag and the condoms back under the pillow.

'Don't you think they'll notice, Dad?' Chook asks.

'They're not going to complain about stolen weed, are they? Anyway, they'll blame the other people in the camping area and rip into them first,' Kev laughs.

Even the thought of weed makes him cheerful.

They go over to the two campervans, parked so close together they look like family. In the annexe of the first van they strike it lucky. On a little card table, neatly set up with an embroidered cloth, is a jar of instant coffee, a loaf of fresh bread and some vegemite. Bingo! The whole lot goes into Chook's bag.

'We've done well,' Kev says. 'I reckon that'll do for our first go.'

He's dying for a joint and a cup of coffee, Chook can see. At least it might make him nicer. They haven't gone into the last campervan but Kev says it's good to leave one for next time. Also, he says, if it's the only one not hit, its owners might get the blame.

Chook asks to go to the toilet before they go back to the campsite.

Kev hesitates, then laughs, shaking his head.

'I don't know what's so good about that bloody

toilet. You've been dying to go in there ever since we arrived.'

Chook thinks he shouldn't even have to ask. It'll be clean. No squatting. No flies buzzing you. Toilet paper and soap. Not like that mosque yard, where he would have had to try to dig it in with his bare hands and wouldn't have been able to wipe his bum. Gross. No wonder he didn't go.

Kev finally agrees, as long as he's quick. They head towards it, scaring a roo out of the paddock surrounding the toilet block. It hops over to the wire fence and clears it in one bound.

The toilet gate is a metal grille and everything inside is stainless steel, even the mirrors. It's clean and dry, with the sun streaming in. There are two showers and two toilets. They go into adjoining cubicles and Chook has his first crap in a toilet for three days, since they left the farm. He hears his father peeing, then going out to wash his hands.

'There's no soap!' Kev calls to him.

Chook doesn't care now. They've got most of what they wanted out of the camping ground.

'The showers are solar heated,' Kev calls again to Chook, who is still sitting on the toilet, making it last. 'I seen the panels on the roof outside. They'd be beautiful on a day like this but I reckon we better clear out. We've got our waterhole anyway.'

Yeah, thinks Chook, but you come out of that smelling like a swamp hen.

Outside, his dad is singing a rude song while he waits for Chook, probably thinking about the love nest where he scored the weed.

'Wild thing! I think I love you. Take down your pants and let me know for sure . . .'

That's when they hear a V8 pulling up outside the toilet block. They hear car doors banging one after the other and the sound of voices. Chook is too scared to move. He hears Kev step into one of the shower cubicles and click the lock shut. The next thing he registers is the outside metal gate opening, then banging shut. Someone has come in.

The man goes into the second toilet cubicle and locks it, clearing his throat loudly. Chook hears him taking down his trousers and easing himself onto the seat. Then he hears him having a crap. It's loud and long and heavy. The kind of crap where his dad would say that somebody must have lowered it with a rope. Chook almost gets the giggles when he thinks of that. The smell of it fills the room. It's like a dead cow.

Then Chook hears a sound on the wall near him. It's a tapping sound and a woman's voice says: 'Ron? Are you there? Can you hear me?'

'What is it?'

Ron's voice is tired, as if he's answered once too often.

'There's no soap in here, Ron. Have you got any there?'

'I'll have a look when I get out.'

There is no soap. Chook knows that.

Ron's groanings come to an end and he tears off paper to wipe. Then he slowly pulls up his clothes, wheezing. Chook can hear him zipping and buttoning as he comes out of the cubicle and calls back to the woman on the other side of the wall.

'No soap here either, Val.'

'That's very poor. I'll have to let the rangers know.'

Ron turns on the tap to rinse his hands and then Chook hears him pull out some paper to dry them. He seems to use the same paper to blow his nose loudly. Chook stays where he is. The shower is running in his dad's cubicle. He wonders if he really is having a shower. Then he hears Ron leave, banging the door after him. His wife joins him outside the toilet block, still complaining about soap, and then their voices die away as they get into their car and the throb of the engine takes over.

Chook is scared. Where are they from? The tents or the campervans? They don't sound like the sort of people to have weed and condoms under their pillows. More likely they're the ones with the tablecloth and the bread and vegemite. The sort that'd know exactly when something has been touched. What if they find out immediately and come looking for them? He unlocks the door quickly and hears his dad doing the same. They both come out. His dad's jeans are wet from running the shower.

'Bastard water splashed all over me,' his dad says grimly. He checks to see if the bag has stayed dry. Luckily the zipper was done up and the food looks fine. Better than fine. Totally scrumptious.

'What'll we do, Dad, if they come after us?'

'I don't think they'll notice it straight off. But come on, hurry up and we'll go back through the scrub, so they don't see us.'

The two of them go out, his dad peering through the gate before they emerge. There is no sign of the couple at first, but as they come out they see a Ford Falcon pulled up over beside the brownish tent. So that's where they're from. Ron and Val are sitting at the table with the esky at their feet. They haven't opened it yet. Chook feels a pang of jealousy. That fully loaded esky.

He can hear Val's voice going on at Ron again, but they're too far away to hear what she's saying. Probably still on about soap. As if that's the rangers' problem. They've got more important things to do than put soap in the toilet block. They're not cleaners.

Chook and Kev slip round the back of the building and scurry silently along the creek bank the same way they drove their car early that morning, without passing through the camping ground. Chook turns once to look at the couple. He can only see the back of them and doesn't think they've spotted him and his dad. He turns round, tripping over tree roots in his eagerness to get back and start eating. It's lucky Ron and Val didn't turn up a few moments earlier. They would have caught them red-handed.

'Bastards should have gone on the tour,' his dad is muttering. 'No bloody interest in Koori history. I bet they vote Liberal.'

Chook thinks about the people on the tour getting to see all the Koori stuff. One day he'll come back and take that tour. But right now, his stomach is asking for more chocolate biscuits. Bacon and eggs. Cheese and vegemite on bread. A Coke. He fixes his eyes on the magical black bag his dad is carrying. Things are looking up. As long as Ron and Val don't come snooping down the creek looking for them.

Row after row the bikes gleamed at him, new and powerful. They smelt of rubber and fresh grease. Max had left the ute parked right outside the shop, and Chook could see Terror hanging half out of the back, desperate to join them.

One bike caught Chook's eye straight away. A mountain bike, his size exactly, mounted above him on a stand. It was mostly shiny black, but red and yellow flames blazed out from its frame and sparked down the forks connecting the handles to the rest of the bike.

Max read: 'Striker!' The gold name written in the flames. The handles reared up high, their ends covered in easy grips for his hands. He gazed at it in awe.

'Get on it! See how it feels,' Max urged him.

He climbed up on the seat, spun the pedals and pressed the brakes. It felt perfect. Exactly what he needed. Max had said when they got out of the ute that he could have any bike in the shop, no matter what it cost.

'It'll be like an early Christmas present,' he said.

When Chook jumped on him to thank him, he almost knocked him over on the footpath and a few people passing by turned to look.

'Oh gawd,' Max said. 'You don't know your own strength.'

Terror thought they were playing and barked at them from the ute, keen to join in.

Now Max was waiting for him to make up his mind. Which one would it be?

It was a hard choice but mountain bikes were best for mountains, Chook thought, and mountains were what they had round the farm. He did a final check round all the shiny rows, the shop owner following in case he wanted any special features explained, but he had made up his mind.

'This one,' he said, pointing at Striker.

'Done!' said Max, taking out his wallet to pay. Once he had the money, the shop owner grinned and whispered to Chook that he'd chosen the best bike in the shop. They got it down off the stand and Chook wheeled it out to the ute, where Max helped him lift it into the back without getting a single scratch on it. They roped it upright to the sides of the ute. Chook wanted to climb on and sit on it all the way home to the farm, but Max said the cops in town wouldn't appreciate it and made him come in the front with him and Terror, who licked him all over his face.

'Git down,' Max growled at Terror.

All the way home Chook kept looking behind him at the bike, riding like a proud warrior in the back of the ute. Striker. His first new bike ever.

The minute they got home he unroped his bike from the back of the ute, lifted it down with Max's help, jumped on it and tore off without saying goodbye to Max. He rode without stopping, across rough tracks, down moist gullies and up impossible hills. It was night by the time he came home, exhausted.

His dad was waiting for him.

'You can't keep it,' he said. Chook's world went dark. 'What's he doing spending that sort of money on you? He still reckons he can't afford to pay me what he owes me.'

Then Chook begged as he'd never begged before. Please, please, please, he had to keep it. It was a Christmas present. It was the first new bike he had ever, ever, had. He showed his dad the special handles, the flames, the name.

Kev must have seen how much it meant to him. He hesitated, looking at Chook with a worried face, then said: 'OK, keep it, but that's all you're getting for Christmas.'

Chook didn't care. It was all he wanted. He brought the bike inside and parked it in the lounge room next to his bed, so he could look at it while he went to sleep. Striker. Proud warrior. He hung his cap on the handlebars and thought about where he'd ride it the next day. There were heaps of places he still wanted to explore.

His dad paused on his way past to the bedroom.

'Nice unit,' he said and ruffled Chook's hair.

It was, Chook thought. A very nice unit.

CHAPTER TWELVE

THE GAS

As soon as they get back, his dad empties all the food out onto the ground. Chook's fingers are itching to reach out and grab it, but his dad says first they should repack his clothes in the bag, in case they have to make a run for it, if Ron and Val or anyone else shows. He's right, Chook knows, picking up the clothes scattered everywhere and shoving them in any old how, but that food is begging to be eaten.

They start with the chocolate biscuits, sharing the whole packet and looking at each other in surprise when they're gone. Then they pig out on fresh bread with cheese and vegemite and Coke, saving the bacon and eggs for their tea. The fizzy Coke goes up Chook's nose just the way he likes it. His stomach stops hurting and growling and begins to feel warm, settled and thankful.

His dad puts the leftover food away in his bag, to spoil the fun of the ants and flies which came in droves as soon as they started eating, and to hide the evidence if anyone comes looking. Then he rolls a joint and draws it in deep. 'It's good weed,' he says, when he finally lets out his breath. He should know, the amount he's had, Chook thinks. They sit in silence for a while, enjoying the peaceful afternoon. Even the apostle birds have gone off to fight and fuss and play happy families somewhere else so it seems that the sun beats down on Kev and Chook alone in the whole world.

'Nice, ain't it,' Kev says. 'Peaceful. As long as they all leave us alone. I wouldn't care if I never saw another soul. Just you and me, forever, eh, Chook?'

Chook doesn't answer. It would be sort of good, but he knows it's not going to happen that way.

His dad starts laughing.

'I was just thinking . . . Did I ever tell you about the first time I ever seen a steam train?'

'No.'

'I was riding me bike, it was when I was living with my dad, and I must have come to a railway track, and suddenly I seen this monster coming whooshing and steaming along the track. I didn't know what the hell it was. I nearly shat myself. Dropped me bike and ran! Had to come back later and find the bike and ask me dad what the monster was. He told me it was something called a steam train! We'd never been nowhere near one up till then. Steam train. Must have been one of the last on that line. Big smoky dragon!' He laughs and laughs.

Chook says: 'Didn't I used to call trains "franes"?'

'Yep. You couldn't say tr ... franes and frousers ...'

Chook starts laughing too. 'And frucks, Dad!'

'I thought you was swearing at somebody when you yelled out "look at that fruck"!'

They both laugh. Then Chook thinks of another joke: 'Why won't a cannibal eat a clown, Dad?'

Kev shrugs, still smiling. 'Dunno. Why won't a cannibal eat a clown?'

'Because he thinks they taste funny! Where would you find a dog with no legs?'

'Where you left him.'

'That's right!'

He must have asked him that one before.

'My turn,' his dad says. 'A bloke went to a fancy-dress party with a woman sitting on his shoulders. When people asked him what he'd come as, he said: "A tortoise". "What's the woman doing on your shoulders?" they asked. "Oh," he said, that's Michelle."'

Chook wrinkles his nose. 'What's funny about that?'

'Michelle. Get it? Me shell?'

Now Chook gets it. Not that it's funny.

His dad tries another one: 'A brain and a pair of jumper leads went into a bar and ordered some beers

189

but the barman wouldn't serve them. "Why won't you serve us?" they asked. "Because one of you is out of your head," he said, "and the other one's about to start something!'"

They both love that one. They roll around laughing till it hurts. Then it's Chook's turn.

'What do you call a man with no arms or legs lying in a pile of leaves?'

'Dunno,' his dad says.

'Russell.'

His dad laughs again and keeps on laughing longer than Chook expects. Let's face it, when he's stoned, he laughs at a fly going by.

When he finally stops, Kev asks: 'What's the joke that keeps an idiot in suspense?'

Chook tries to think.

His dad waits and waits. Then he punches him on the arm and says: 'Gotcha!'

'Hang on,' Chook says, 'I haven't given up yet.'

'Don't you get it? You're the idiot in suspense.'

Chook doesn't see what's funny about that. There's no need for his dad to turn nasty when things are beginning to go well. He turns his back on Kev and moves away. After a while, Kev calls out that it's four o'clock. Chook shrugs. So what?

Kev says: 'The tour should be getting back soon. By dark, at any rate. The rangers'll be bringing the gas.

And the happy campers will be finding out what they've lost and maybe coming to look for it. The way we're going, there'll be bugger all left by then.'

Chook lies down with his head on his bag and pulls his hat down over his eyes, blocking out his dad. He thinks the smell of the hat is gradually fading. He's tired now that he's full of food. He crosses his fingers that nobody comes looking for them. There'd be no point anyway. There's no way they'll get their food back, now it's eaten.

He's sitting at a table. It seems to be the table at the farm because his new bike, Striker, is right beside him. It's tea time and there's food on the plate in front of him. Lamb shanks again. He's starving. He goes to pick up his knife and fork to start eating but every time he tries they bury themselves deep in the table, the way ticks burrow into your neck. After a few goes, he decides to take them by surprise. When he pounces on the fork suddenly, it tries its old tricks but he gets it before it can go in deep. He pulls it up but it scares the shit out of him, howling like a wounded dog, and when he looks down at the table, there is a pool of blood in the place where the fork was lying.

Around five o'clock, when they hear cars returning to the camping ground, both of them go on the alert. They pick up the sound of the rangers' four wheel drive heading their way and wait for them to show up. Then they realise it is going along the road, not the creek bank. The sound gets further and further away, then disappears over in the direction of the rangers' house.

'They must have forgotten,' Kev says.

'I'm starving,' Chook says. It's true too. He's already hungry again.

Kev says: 'Bugger it. Let's light the fire.'

Chook can't get over how quickly the wood catches. Dead finish. Probably because it's been lying around on the hot, dry ground forever. Back at the farm, they would sometimes be cursing and blowing on it and screwing up newspaper for hours before the wood caught alight. That was the only heating they had and the winter was really cold. Mornings were the worst. Chook got chilblains on his hands and feet. His dad said they came from toasting them too close to the fire and making them turn hot too quickly. Max got chilblains too and said the fire wasn't the problem. The cold was.

The bacon jumps and sizzles and curls up at the edges, and the egg spreads out over the bottom of the billy like a great white cloak round a golden head. Chook is nearly drooling, watching it cook. His dad gives him the first serve and then does another lot for himself. Chook soaks the bread in the yolk and slops it down his chin. It is like eating sunshine.

His dad finishes cooking his and they eat till they are full. In fact their tummies must have shrunk, because it doesn't take long for them to feel stuffed, lying around gagged out. Usually when his dad is stoned, he can eat five hamburgers, easy.

'I'm surprised,' Kev says, shaking his head, 'that they didn't show up. It ain't like Koories to let ya down.'

Kev has been holding off having a coffee, waiting for the gas, but now he says he can't wait any longer and goes down to the creek to rinse out the billy and get some more water.

While he's away, Chook hears a four wheel drive coming along the bank, its headlights piercing the dark. He recognises the sound of the rangers' car and feels relieved. They haven't let them down after all. His dad spoke too soon.

Kev hears it too and comes hurrying back from the creek just as the car pulls up and Reg and Lyall get out.

'Sorry about the fire, mate,' Kev calls to them as they come over. 'We couldn't wait. The boy was starving.'

'No worries,' Reg says. 'We got held up.'

Lyall is carrying a small gas stove and cylinder which he puts down on the ground near Kev. Reg has a carton of stubbies which he also dumps near the fire.

'Do you want me to put the fire out? I was just gunna make a coffee,' says Kev, eyeing off the beers.

'Leave it!' Reg says. 'We brought you some stubbies. Uncle Cliff said it was too late to go looking for pituri now. Maybe tomorrow.'

Kev quickly passes up the coffee in favour of a beer and they all sit down round the fire again.

Chook notices they seem to like having the fire going, even though they're not supposed to. Of course they would. They are Koories after all. His dad told him Koories used to sleep with a fire between them and sometimes roll into it in their sleep, which scared Chook off camping even more. He always imagined himself waking up burnt. He wonders if Reg and Lyall have rolled into any fires lately. He inspects them covertly for any sign of burns but their skin looks all smooth and shiny.

Reg gives Kev and Lyall a beer and knocks the top off one for himself. Chook asks where their uncle is.

'Gone home. He just comes out to help us with the tour. He's got a place back there in Wilcannia. His daughter took him back a little while ago.'

Lyall smacks his lips over the first stubbie and reckons he deserves it.

'I've been on track maintenance all arvo,' he says, 'down on the old gorge track. Stinking hot, mate, and they sent us this goose from Sydney, this trainee ranger. He done nothing but sit down in the shade. Every time I looked round, he was sitting on his arse, so I told him to go and clear the dead goats out of the rock pool.'

Reg laughs and explains for Kev and Chook's benefit. 'That's standard, mate. That's what we always get 'em to do. Young goats fall off the side of the gorge and get drowned in the pool.'

Lyall adds: 'You don't have to do nothing about it, because flooding clears 'em out eventually. But he didn't know that. Spent all the rest of the afternoon dragging through the pool. Bloody water stinks to high heaven.'

Chook can imagine it. He's got a lot of sympathy for the trainee ranger.

Lyall laughs again. 'I tell you what. Them rookies from Sydney . . . Fair game, mate.'

Kev laughs too. 'Nappy rash, eh?'

'Too right. But we fix 'em, eh, Reg?'

'Fix 'em good, cuz,' Reg says, draining the stubbie.

Chook asks if he found any dead goats.

'Not one, Chook,' Lyall says. 'Not one. Pity, eh!'

The men all laugh again.

Lyall says he cleared some fallen rocks and branches from the walking track.

'Red river gums,' he says, looking up at the ones above their heads. Chook follows his gaze. 'They're buggers for dropping their branches on tourists' heads. Tends to put them off coming back. You want to watch out with them lot.'

Kev says he'll take his chances but Chook moves further away. With his luck, he'll be the one that gets hit.

Lyall sucks on the last of his beer.

'Yeah … summer's the best time in this job,' he says. 'Not too many tourists and plenty of time to sit down with Uncle Cliff and learn stuff. Like I just seen something down the track I think might be an ochre bowl. I'll bring him down there and show him, see what he thinks.'

'There must be a lot of stuff like that out here,' Kev says.

'Yeah,' says Reg, 'heaps. And now we own it, people can't come and take them away for souvenirs like they used to. Bastards.'

'I had a job once in Tasmania,' says Kev, 'working for the Tasmanian Aboriginal Centre. We went on these big treks into the mountains on foot, looking for tools and that and listing all the stuff we found. Best job I ever had.'

Chook hates remembering that time when his dad was away in the mountains. He left Chook with his girlfriend at the time, who was really mean. Her name was Jasmine and she kept telling people in front of him that she didn't want to be saddled with the kid. It seemed months till his dad came back to collect him but Kev said it was only two weeks. The longest two weeks of Chook's life so far.

It was Jasmine that made them leave in the end. She lent them her car to drive while she went over to see her sister in Melbourne. What she didn't tell them was that it was stolen. Chook and his dad were driving through Launceston when the cops pulled them over and did a check on the engine number. His dad told them that he was only borrowing it from a friend, but they didn't believe him. They charged him with stealing it and his dad had to do a runner before the court case came up.

'Were youse living down that way?'

'For a while,' says Kev.

'Bloody cold,' says Reg.

Kev says: 'Mate, we loved it. Out there in the mountains you could do your own thing without nobody hassling you.'

'Nah,' says Reg. 'Give me the heat and flies and the dust and the desert. This is the only place that feels like home. Eh, Lyall?'

Lyall nods and grunts as he leans over to get three more beers for the men.

Chook asks Reg, while he can get a word in, if he took people to see the hand prints today.

'Course I did,' he says. 'Funny mob they were. Real eager to ask questions. One woman wanted to know why we never grew crops. "Why bother," I said, "when the earth gives us everything we need?"'

Chook likes that. It's what his dad tells him about. Mother Earth taking care of her children, and her children taking care of Mother Earth in return. That's what people aren't doing now, Kev always says.

'Another one asked me if I still used a stone axe to chop wood. I told her I wasn't bloody stupid. It's a lot quicker cutting the stuff up with a chainsaw.'

'What? They think you still live in the fuckin stone age?' Kev asks.

'Some of them do. Most of them are pretty ignorant. Still, the ones that come on the tour at least have got the right attitude. They all think the bloody government should say sorry to us.'

Chook thinks it should too. 'Sorry' isn't a hard word to say. He always seems to be saying it to his dad. Not that his dad says it very often to him.

'Especially the stolen generation, eh. My wife is one of the stolen generation, mate, and she is real bitter. Real bitter about what she's missed out on.'

'Like a lot of us, bro,' his dad says.

'Just being out here, you feel better, though,' Reg says. 'You only got to look up at the stars and see how huge it all is and how small we are. Mate, we're nothing.'

They all look up at the stars now coming out in a vast silvery display. Chook is looking for the Southern Cross, as he always does, and then for the saucepan with the handle, when Lyall nudges him.

'See them six bright stars together up there, Chook? There used to be seven, you know. The seven sisters we called 'em.'

'What happened to the other sister?' Chook asks.

'She come down to earth and become one of our first parents.'

'Did Uncle Cliff tell you that?' Chook asks.

'Everybody round here knows that story. I dunno where I heard it first,' Lyall says.

'One of them stories handed down through the age,' Reg adds. Chook looks up at the six stars clustering together like little sisters and thinks he'll always remember it.

The men finish two rounds of beers before Reg says they have to go. There are things they've got to finish off before settling in for a night with the AFL on TV. The Crows are playing against Port Adelaide. A big home-town clash for the start of the footie season.

Chook begins to ask if he can come and watch too, thinking it will give him a chance to tell them about Dr Khan, but his dad cuts him off.

'See you soon, then. And thanks for the gas, bro,' he says, looking warningly at Chook.

Reg says he'll leave the other stubbies behind for Kev.

'You're a champ,' Kev says to him.

Chook sidles up to Reg as they are putting the empties in the vehicle and asks: 'Have you got a phone at your place?'

'Sure have,' Reg says. 'Who did you want to ring? Your mum?'

Kev hears the last bit.

'What's he want?' he asks Reg. 'Getting homesick, is he?'

'Sounds like it, mate.'

'Don't worry about it. He'll be OK. We'll ring home tomorrow and keep his mum sweet.'

'Hooroo, Geoff. Hooroo, Chook!' Reg climbs into the vehicle next to Lyall and they take off along the bank and disappear into the night.

Kev turns on Chook: 'Why was you asking about a phone?'

'I wasn't,' says Chook.

'Yes you was. I heard you.'

'I want to ring the Flying Doctors,' says Chook defiantly. 'I'm worried about Dr Khan. What if nobody's found her yet?'

'Somebody would've gone looking for her when she didn't turn up at work. There's bound to be somebody knows where to look. That's why we've got to lie low. Once they find her, she'll give the game away for sure.'

'She's only been here for three weeks.'

'Stop worrying about her, for Christ's sake. Fuckin nosy parker.'

'She wasn't. I asked her to go back and help Max. It was me who —'

'Let it go, Chook, we've been over it. I didn't hurt her hardly at all. She'll live.'

Chook thinks that's what he said about Max and it wasn't true then.

Kev gets the stove linked up to the gas cylinder and lights it. He puts the billy on the stove for coffee. While he waits for it to boil, he rolls another joint.

'I'm going to sleep well tonight,' he tells Chook. 'Pot, beer, a good feed. They're great blokes, ain't they? Share everything. Top blokes.'

Chook doesn't want to talk to his dad any more. He looks round. It's very black now their fire is nearly out. He can already hear sounds he doesn't like. Rustlings and hoppings.

'Roos,' says Kev, listening too, as he has a toke on the joint and a suck of the coffee, then lies back on the ground. Now he's stoned he doesn't seem to feel the lump on his head. 'What a life, eh?'

'I wisht I could go and watch the footie.' Chook is still defiant.

'This is better than bloody TV. You can make up your own program out here. Look at them stars. It's fuckin magnificent. I don't know why anyone would want to be stuck inside a house blocking out the sky on a night like this.'

Chook hopes the night's program won't include wild dogs hiding behind trees and pouncing on him whenever he shuts his eyes. Even though he is angry with his dad, he rolls as close as he can to him.

'And you keep forgetting we're on the bloody run,' Kev goes on. 'We can't get too cosy with anybody. You might be watching the TV and they put our pictures up there on the news or something. How's that going to look? Eh?'

'You said Koories wouldn't give us up.'

'No they wouldn't, but it would put them in a bloody awkward position. Dead set.'

Chook knows he's right. He shuts his eyes for a moment and realises how tired he is. It's been a long day since Dr Khan woke him up early this morning. She must have been lying in the mosque all day with that tape on her mouth and her hands pulled tight behind her, if nobody's come looking. It will be hard for her to sleep. Then he thinks about Max and whether he might wake up from his long sleep tonight. He hopes he isn't in his grave yet.

Suddenly he hears breathing sounds close by. He clutches at his dad.

'What was that?' he says.

'What was what?' Kev answers.

'I heard breathing. Just over there.'

'Some little animal,' Kev says cheerfully. 'Don't worry about it. There's nothing big enough to eat you.'

Chook doesn't know if that's supposed to cheer him up. Wild dogs might not eat him but they could certainly do a lot of damage. It could even be fatal. Chook shivers and moves still closer to his dad.

'Christ, you need a wash! When did you change them clothes?'

Chook realises he hasn't changed since he left the farm. The forced swim in the waterhole has added to the smell.

'I'll change them in the morning,' he says, still pressing close to his dad.

'What are you trying to do?' Kev asks. 'I'll be in the ashes next.'

Then you'd know he was a Koori, Chook thinks. He'd have the burns to prove it.

'You're scared, aren't you, you little bum,' Kev says, messing up his hair.

'I'm not a bum,' Chook says.

'No,' says Kev. 'You're the underpants.'

Chook punches him for that, hard, on the arm holding the joint. That does it. It's on for young and old. His dad puts down his coffee, stubs out the joint, then hits him back. They have a good rumble with punching and kicking and 'is that the best you can do!'

and 'try this then!' Chook gets him a couple of good ones. He also gets hurt a couple of times but he doesn't let on. When he's had enough, he moves away from his dad and sits down on his bag, rubbing his battered ribs and catching his breath. He sees his dad relight the roach and draw the smoke in, releasing it slowly.

'Where are we going to sleep?' Chook asks his dad.

'What's wrong with right here? Under the stars.'

'I'm cold,' Chook says. It feels as if the temperature has dived ten degrees at least since the sun went down.

'Put your coat over you,' Kev says, 'and make a pillow with some of your clothes. Do I have to show you everything? Like the other night in the park.'

Chook finds his coat and pulls it over him, but the ground under him is so cold he feels it seeping through in spite of the coat.

A late bird suddenly squawks and makes him jump.

'Shut up,' Kev shouts at it. 'You're meant to be asleep.'

'It must be a night owl. Like you, Dad.'

His dad is a real night owl and often stays up till three or four in the morning watching TV. No matter what time Chook wakes up in the night, he'll find his dad's eyes wide open, even when he has to get up early on the farm. He says he doesn't need much sleep. Chook does. His eyes are getting heavy in spite of the danger. He feels his dad's arm come over and his hand strokes Chook's cheek, then gently closes his eyes for him.

'Go to sleep,' his dad says. 'Nothing's going to hurt you while I'm here.'

Chook knows he's right. He lets his eyes stay closed. Even stoned, his father will be protecting him. He can count on that. But the cold is in his bones now and his whole body is shaking. No matter how close he gets to his dad, he can't get warm. Then he realises his dad is shaking as well. They're both clattering like a pair of maracas.

'Dad,' he shivers, 'can I sleep in the car?'

'Why not,' his dad says suddenly. 'Maybe I'll come too. It's fuckin freezing, ain't it.'

Chook is up before his dad can change his mind. Throwing on his coat and trying to see where he's putting his feet in the dark, he hurries over to the unlocked car and gets in the front. His dad follows him, bringing his jacket and a couple of shirts that he shoves down over the gap between the front seats to make it more comfortable for Chook.

Kev opens a stubby, the malty smell of beer strong in the car, as he settles down in the back, the short seat making him bend his long frame almost in half. He's so stoned he doesn't care, pulling his jacket over him and giggling softly to himself when he almost falls off, swigging at the beer. He's finished the beer and is asleep and snoring before Chook begins to drop off, warming up only slowly on the car's velour seats. He can still see the six sisters through the car window, watching over him.

His dad is lying on a metal bed all tied down. There are belts on his arms and legs. He has had his last meal of chicken and chips and told Chook he is going to shit all over them if they hang him. They don't hang him. They've decided to give him a lethal injection. He is hooked up to medical stuff like in a hospital. A priest comes and asks him if he's got something to confess. 'Nah,' says his dad. 'He deserved it and I'm not sorry.'

Chook gives him a long hug and refuses to leave him. They eventually have to drag him away into another room where he can see everything that's happening through a glass wall. His dad turns his head and looks at him. Any minute they are going to give him the shot. Chook smashes the glass in front of him and dives through it to rescue his dad. He scrabbles at the belts holding his dad down and almost gets one undone before they haul him away. 'Too late, sonny,' they say. 'Your dad's gone.'

CHAPTER THIRTEEN

BREAKDOWN

When Chook wakes at first light, the bird chorus is deafening. He lies for a moment seeing pink birds flit in and out of trees, wondering where he is. Then he remembers. His body is stiff from sleeping across the gap between the seats. Something is sticking into his hip. He is really cold. The sun hasn't started to warm the car up yet. He wraps his coat tight round him and half sits up, turning to look at his dad asleep behind him. He's lying on his back with his knees bent. He's got his mouth open, snoring loudly. He only does that when he's stoned or drunk. He'll probably sleep for hours yet.

Chook moves across and sits in the driver's seat, turning the steering wheel round this way and that. Then he puts the car into neutral and back into park. He wonders idly where the keys are. Sometimes his dad lets him drive. He used to let him sit on his lap and steer in the beginning and then he let him change gears. On the farm he sometimes drove a few hundred metres on his own, though he had trouble seeing over the dashboard. He looks back again at his dad. Turning on the car's engine will wake his dad for sure and he doesn't think he can steer it along the lumpy creek bank.

He thinks about walking over to the rangers' house and making the phone call before his dad gets up. The trouble is, once they find Dr Khan they'll come looking for his dad even harder, and what will become of him if they catch his dad? But what if Dr Khan dies as well as Max? His dad will never get out of prison then and what about the broken bodies waiting for Dr Khan to save them. What if they die, too? It all makes his brain hurt. He can't decide what to do.

He reaches over and opens the glove box, and sees Dr Khan's makeup jumbled in there. He gets out the tube of lipstick. It has a black top, which he pulls off, and he finds the lipstick hiding in the bottom half. He twists it, watching the dark red tube slowly come up, like a lollipop, towards him. He twists it back down. It reminds him of the way the pink part of a dog's dick comes in and out. He twists it up again, smiling to himself at the thought.

He used to watch Dianne put on lipstick. She used to spread it on the top lip, then the bottom one, then she would rub her lips together backwards and forwards. Finally she would lick her lips slowly with her pink tongue. When he asked her why she did that, she said it fixed the lipstick in place. She used to tease him when she caught him watching, exaggerating the licking, pushing her tongue well out and running its tip slowly round her mouth. It was gross in a way, but it made him feel sort of tickly. She would finish off by bringing her red lips together and blowing him a kiss.

'You little perve,' she'd say and mess up his hair.

He glances back at his dad to check he is still asleep, then brings the tube up to his mouth and looks in the car mirror. Very slowly, he draws a broad line of red along his top lip and another line along his bottom lip. He rubs his lips together backwards and forwards. It's harder to stay on the line than Dianne made it look. He smudges it over the edges, but it is a beautiful colour. Like the red wine Max drank out of the cask. Max used to offer him a sip but it was sour and he spat it out. He puts his tongue out and licks slowly along the bottom and the top lip, just like Dianne did. It tastes better than he thought it would. Better than red wine anyway.

He looks in the mirror again. The red lips make his skin look darker. He pushes them forward and pouts like Dianne. He turns the collar of his coat up like she used to and blows a kiss to his image in the mirror, making a slight popping noise. He twists the lipstick again to make it go down and puts it back in the glove box. Next, he chooses some eye shadow in a case with a see-through lid. It's blue and powdery. He takes out a little brush and strokes some on his eyelids, half closing his eyes to see the result in the mirror. It's the colour of the sky and makes his hazel eyes turn blue. He looks like a pretty girl. Like Dianne, only better! He flutters his eyelids a few times.

When he opens his eyes fully, his dad's face is beside his in the mirror. The look on his face is pure rage. His head looks as though it has swollen up to twice its size and his eyes flash black. Next minute, the mirror image disappears as his dad hauls him into the back seat, pulling him through the opening between the seats. The eye shadow falls to the floor as his dad screams right in his face.

'What the fuck are you doing? What the fuck? What are you? A fag? A pansy? Wipe that fuckin stuff off right now.'

His dad tightens his hold on the front of his T-shirt and begins rubbing it hard on his eyes and lips. It won't all come off and that seems to infuriate him even more. He starts hitting at Chook, hard hits this time on his cheeks and mouth, not playful, like in last night's rumble. As he hits, he curses him. 'Little fuckin faggot' and 'fuckin girl'. Chook has blood running down his face. He can taste it in his mouth. He tries feebly to fight back but his dad is in a fury.

Finally Kev opens the car door and flings Chook out onto the ground.

'Go and have a wash, you filthy cunt,' he says and slams the car door shut.

Chook gets himself up with difficulty and walks down to the waterhole on shaky legs. He bends down and sees his face all bloody and swollen in the water. He splashes some on his eyes and mouth, feeling them sting. He rubs as much as he can off without making it worse. Then he slumps down on the sand and gives up.

He doesn't know how long he lies there. His dad does not come near him. He can hear his dad in the distance, getting out of the car and moving round. Chook lies as still as Max did the last time he saw him. He wants to be dead too.

Chook was yawning like a bear in winter when Max suggested he have a bath and go to sleep in the big bed. Max said he'd stay and wait for Kev to come home. It was the usual Saturday night. They had played cars and cards and watched TV. When it got late, Max always made sure the door was locked and Chook was asleep or close to it, then left, whether his dad was home or not. Tonight he ran a bath for Chook and filled it up nearly to the top. It was scalding hot when he lowered himself into it bit by bit, getting used to the burning.

Max went away while he floated the Camaro and the Hummer across a flooded river and managed to land them on the opposite bank. Max came back in and asked if he'd washed his ears. Chook said he had.

Max said: 'I bet you haven't!' and looked in both of them. Filthy! He got a washer and soap and did Chook's ears for him and then his back. It was nice, feeling the soap swishing on his skin, Max's touch gentle.

When he felt Max's hands reach down and touch his willy and then rub soap on it, that seemed nice too. Very nice. He felt him stroke and rub him. He could hear Max's breathing getting loud but couldn't see his face because Max was behind him. He could smell his sheep smell.

Suddenly Max stopped and took his hands away. Chook didn't dare speak or turn and look at him. He heard him go out of the room. Chook blinked. He felt strange, not sure if it had really happened. He couldn't hear Max now. Maybe he had locked the door and gone home.

He got out of the bath and dried himself quickly, then went through the lounge room, past Striker standing guard beside his bed, without seeing any sign of Max. Picking up two handfuls of cars to take with him, he went into the bedroom, turned on the light and hopped into his dad's bed. He loved its sagging-in-the-middle mattress and warm bedclothes. He put some of his cars under the pillow and arranged some on the floor beside him, then settled down and shut his eyes.

He heard Max come in from somewhere and turn off the light. He must have been outside. Then he could feel Max standing next to him, beside the bed.

'Good night,' Max said softly.

Chook muttered 'Night', turned over and waited for Max to leave. A while passed before he heard him move away and there was a rustling sound in the corner near the chair. When he felt Max climb into the bed next to him, he was half pleased. Comforted but nervous. Guilty. He lay unnaturally still, turned on his side away from him. He felt Max's body press against his. Max was naked and bony. His hard willy was against Chook's back. It was uncomfortable and Max's breathing was loud again, like in the bathroom.

Chook moved away, struggling to get out of the middle. Max did not follow him. He felt Max turn over, away from him. Chook lay still, not daring to make a sound. He heard Max's breathing getting quieter. Gradually Chook calmed down and finally slept.

★ ★ ★

When flies start to buzz him and the sun's warmth begins to revive him in spite of himself, he sits up, anger growing. How dare his dad beat him up for nothing. Just like he beat Max up for nothing and tied Dr Khan up for trying to help. How dare he drag him round like this, taking him away every time he starts to feel at home. He looks down and sees the leather anklet he wears to match his dad's. He reaches down and pulls at its flimsy ties, ripping it off and throwing it down in the sand.

Then he gets up and looks back towards where his dad is lighting the stove. He has his back turned. Silently, Chook crosses the creek and clambers up the bank on the other side.

He knows the general direction of the rangers' house. He hasn't put any shoes on, though, and the ground is full of prickles. He walks along carefully, watching where he puts his feet, trying to avoid the worst of them. He is out of sight of his father now. He can hear a car moving round, over to the left in the camping ground. The rangers' house must be directly behind it, hidden by the high creek banks. He can see a road off to his right but doesn't want to walk there, in case his dad comes driving along looking for him once he realises he's gone.

He surprises a wallaby eating and sees the fear in its eyes before it takes off. He feels sick at the way everything in the world seems to be afraid of everything

214

else. He keeps on going, even though bushes tear at his coat and his feet are getting filled with more and more prickles. He comes to a crossroads, where he can see the tracks of a vehicle heading to the left, while the main road goes straight on. He steps out of the scrub onto the dirt track, sitting down to pull out some of the prickles before he sets off again, following the track left. After about two or three hundred metres, he sees a house with a shiny tin roof. The rangers' white four wheel drive is parked out the front. He goes up to the door and knocks.

There is a long pause and he knocks again, louder. Finally he hears footsteps coming and a woman with black hair and dark skin like Reg opens the door. She's wearing a dressing gown and has a cranky look on her face, as if he's woken her up. She gets a shock when she sees him. He realises he probably still has makeup on, mixed with blood. His face still hurts and he can feel his lip swollen up.

'Is Reg or Lyall here?' he asks.

'They're in bed, love, but come in.'

'I just want to make a phone call.'

'Are you all right?' she says. 'What's happened to your face?'

'It's nothing,' he says. 'Can I use your phone? I want to ring the Flying Doctors.'

'I can do it. Is anyone else hurt?'

'No,' says Chook. 'I've got to do it. I want to tell them something urgent.'

'The phone's in here,' she says, 'but it's only half seven. I'm not sure if anyone . . .'

'They'll be there,' Chook says. Dr Khan rang them early yesterday morning.

He follows the woman into the kitchen where a phone hangs on the wall.

'Have you got the number?' she asks.

'I know it,' he says, taking the phone off the hook and dialling. The woman watches him, as if she is working something out. He turns away when a female voice answers, ready to lower his voice.

'Good morning. Flying Doctor Service.'

'Charlie Hotel Oscar Oscar —'

The woman's voice interrupts him before he can finish: 'Pardon? Who's speaking please?'

Chook gives up on the language. He obviously hasn't got through to the pilot.

'It's about Dr Khan. She's in the old mosque, tied up,' Chook whispers, his voice hoarse from the strain of trying to keep it low.

'Who's calling?' the woman asks again urgently, but Chook hangs up.

There. He's done it. It's the right thing to do, even if she's already been found. If she hasn't, maybe he's saved her life.

'Thanks,' he says to the woman.

'Is that it?' she asks.

'Yeah.'

'What about your face?'

He shrugs.

'Why don't you come and have a wash at least? We got plenty of hot water.'

He shakes his head. 'I've got to go back.'

'Where are you camped?' she asks.

Chook waves vaguely towards the camping ground.

'With your dad?'

Chook nods.

'Yeah, that's right, Reg told me about youse.'

'Are you a relative of his?' Chook asks. She looks like she could be.

She laughs. 'You could say that, love, I'm his missus.'

Chook hasn't imagined Reg with a missus. He seems like a man's man, like his dad.

'Say hi to him and Lyall and Uncle Cliff,' he says, turning to go. He doesn't want his dad to find him there.

'Hang on, don't go. Can I put something on them cuts for you? Your dad beat you up, eh?'

'No,' he says. 'It's all right. I've got to go.'

The woman doesn't want him to leave. 'Hang on a minute. I'll get Reg up,' she says.

'No, I'll be all right.'

He hurries towards the front door which is still open. She follows him.

'Can I give you something to take back and put on your —'

'I'm right,' he says as he steps out. Then he stops suddenly and turns back: 'Oh, who won?'

'Who won what?' she says, screwing up her eyes.

'Last night. The footie.'

'The Crows, I think,' she says.

'Good,' he says. He was going for them because he likes crows. He likes their shiny black feathers and sad cry. Though he doesn't turn back, he knows she is watching him from the doorway as he goes down the track to the crossroads and heads back through the scrub towards their campsite. It is hot walking now and he takes his coat off and carries it.

He thinks about the phone call. He knows he's done a good thing if it means Dr Khan gets free, but it is a bad thing for his dad. It will lead the cops to them. They have to get moving fast. He decides that when he gets back he will make his dad move on. Anywhere would be better than here. Anywhere with shops. The rangers won't give them up, of course, but they can't keep robbing the campers. Sooner or later a posse will come down the creek after them. A lynch mob baying for their blood, like in the old westerns his dad used to get out on video. He can see them now, whipping their horses on as they come through the creek bed, kicking up sand with wild cries and swooping like vultures on their campsite, scattering them and their belongings to the four winds.

His face is still stinging. Flies are starting to discover the dried blood on his cheeks and lips. Chook wonders if his dad will say sorry. It's a pretty safe bet he won't, though he owes it to him. Sometimes, after a belting, although his dad didn't apologise, he did act a lot nicer round him for a while.

He sits down and pulls out some more prickles from his feet when he gets close to the campsite. His feet still hurt even after he pulls them out. He gets up again and walks down the steep bank and across the creek bed. His father is sitting drinking coffee. His eyes are red as if he has smoked another joint.

'Where have you been?' he asks, as Chook comes closer.

'Went for a walk,' Chook says, as briefly as possible.

'Didn't do much of a job cleaning up your face. Still look like a girl.'

Chook doesn't bother answering that. He puts his coat back in his bag, then sits down on it and looks into the distance, back towards the rangers' house.

There is a silence. Then his dad says: 'Do you want some baked beans?'

Chook shakes his head. He has had one baked bean too many.

'What about breakfast? You got to eat.'

Chook says: 'I'm not hungry. My mouth hurts.'

'Course you are. Eat something. Get some bread.'

Chook gets up, takes a piece of bread out of the fresh packet and begins nibbling at it without putting anything on it. It's soft and slips down easily. His dad pours a cup of Coke and hands that to him and he sips at it, trying to avoid the liquid stinging his split lip.

His dad finishes his coffee. Neither of them speak for a while. Then his dad gets up, goes to his bag and starts looking through it. Chook tries to ignore him but half sees him take a bit of rag out and dip it in the water he boiled for coffee. He comes over to Chook and begins to gently wash his face. At first Chook pulls away but his father holds on and keeps on washing. It's hot and it stings. Chook winces each time. His dad puts the wet rag down, gets the towel out and carefully dries off his face. Then Chook sees him look again in the bag and find some mercurochrome, the one coloured purple, not orange, and bring that over. He dips the rag in the bottle and spreads it over the swollen lip and on his cheeks. Tears come into Chook's eyes at the gentleness of the touch, as well as at the stinging, but he fights them back. His dad is not going to see him go weak again.

As Kev finishes and puts away the mercurochrome and the towel, he says: 'Don't put that rubbish on your face again.'

Chook doesn't answer.

'You hear me?'

'I heard you.'

Chook stands up and picks up his bag.

'What are you doing?' his dad asks.

'I'm not staying another night here.'

'Where do you think you're going?'

'Away from here. Somewhere with shops.'

'We can knock off the camping ground again.'

'I don't want to. They'll catch us for sure if we do it again.'

'You leave it to me. I'll decide when we go and when we stay.'

Chook walks over and gets the car keys out of his dad's bag, then turns and goes up to the car. He sees his dad smirk at the thought of him driving away. He opens the hatchback and puts his bag in, taking out the small cars and his cap, which are packed on the top. Kev watches but makes no move to stop him.

As he gets into the driver's seat, Chook picks up the eye shadow that his dad knocked to the floor and puts it back in the glove box, shutting it firmly. He catches a glimpse of his face in the rear vision mirror and gets a shock. His lip is swollen and purple and his cheek dotted with purple bruising. No wonder Reg's missus was worried about him. He glances back at his dad.

Kev is propped up on one elbow, under the dangerous gums, rolling a joint.

Chook puts the key in the ignition and turns it on, hoping the radio will work. He might hear Kylie again or one of the boy bands he used to watch on television with Max. Nothing but static comes out. Nothing works out here. It's the pits. He turns the ignition off again.

He picks up the Chevvy and the Valiant Charger and runs them along the dashboard, vowing not to leave the car or eat again till they get out of here. He has to make a stand now, for both their sakes. The Chevvy burns off the Valiant as they tumble off the dashboard onto the seat and come to grief on the handbrake. He thinks about the rest of his cars lying all alone back at the farm. He's got to get back for them soon.

The best night he ever had when he lived at the farm was the time he and Dianne went to a funfair in Bathurst. His dad was out at the pub, and she was minding Bev's Mirage, so they had wheels, but his dad said they couldn't go out. No reason. He just said he didn't trust her as far as he could throw her. As soon as he left, she looked at Chook like a naughty child and said: 'I'm bored. Let's go, kiddo.'

She drove like a bat out of hell. They roared into Bathurst along the Sofala road, passing the house where there were always sheep lined up, pressing their noses against the windows and doors. Dianne always said Mr and Mrs Mutton lived there. Then they sped past the haunted house where they'd gone looking for treasures with his dad one night and got the shit scared out of them when a storm broke and they thought they saw a dead baby in a cradle that was rocking backwards and forwards. It might have been a doll, but Chook always looked the other way and said 'I hate rabbits' for good luck, when they went past that place.

It was a cold night, but they were rugged up, Chook wearing his new camouflage jacket, as they wandered through cheerful crowds, eating fairy floss. Chook was so pleased to be there, he couldn't help taking little skips every second step along the paths that nestled in the shade of big old trees. He could hear the cries of the show people floating out on the breeze, calling just to him. Every child wins a prize!

'I wonder how fairies get into floss?' Dianne asked, taking a big melting munch of it.

They stopped first at the laughing clowns. When Dianne handed over the money, the toothless showman interrupted himself just long enough to give them the balls. 'Every child wins a . . .' They took turns rolling them into the clowns' dumb open mouths as they swung from side to side, trying to score one of the numbers up on the board. Chook held on to the balls for the longest possible time before releasing them, but no matter how hard he tried he didn't get any of the prize-winning numbers. Neither he nor his dad ever did, but they still gave you a prize anyway. The man handed him a plastic wristwatch for losing. He put it on his wrist, saying it would help him tell the time. Dianne reminded him it was only a toy, but he was sure the hands were moving. She got a plastic comb and brush set, which she dumped in the first bin she saw.

He and Dianne went on all the fastest rides. There was the Giant Octopus, with innards that flashed and legs that went up and down with a vrooming sound, and the Pirate Ship that did 360s, as well as the Mighty Mouse that tore round and round narrow tracks and swooped down sudden wild drops.

When Dianne got off the Mighty Mouse, she said she shouldn't have eaten so much fairy floss. She was sitting down on the ground holding her stomach when Chook spotted the dodgem cars and took off, forgetting Dianne, forgetting everything but the siren song of the cars. As she caught up, still holding the remains of the fairy floss and her stomach, he said: 'Can I? *Please*?'

'Eat the rest of this bloody stuff first,' she said. 'I can't.'

He swallowed the last bits, tasting the bitterness of the pink food dye coming through the sugar. Then

Dianne handed him cash to buy a ticket and sat down on the grass nearby to recover.

'Watch me,' he shouted, as he ran off with the ticket. He had to wait for the ride before to finish and stood as close as he could to the entrance, spellbound by the action, never taking his eyes off the car he wanted. A beautiful, red, low-slung job. He wanted it with all his might. It was everything he had ever wanted.

He watched as the cars spun along in time to the music and the attendant swung from pole to pole, freeing awesome pile-ups and helping little kids by pointing them in the right direction. Girls, Chook noted with disgust. They couldn't drive for nuts and they stopped blokes like himself getting a good run on.

The music stopped. The riders left their cars. His time had come. New riders were free to grab a car. Every child's a winner. Chook burst through the barrier and sped towards his red car. There was no one else in the race. He claimed it with a flying leap, strapped on his belt and waited urgently for the start. This would be the ride of his life. The attendant came round, checking they were ready, and then, yes, they were off, music filling their heads, cars crashing into each other, steering wheels spinning desperately, mouths opening to scream.

Chook wanted to avoid crashes. Not for him this bumping or being bumped. He wanted a clear road with the soft top down, the wind in his hair and the music playing. Smooth. Sweet. He looked for Dianne and gave her a triumphant wave. She was still looking green and gave him a limp wave back.

Just then a little boy in a Batman cape, sitting on his father's lap, sideswiped him, spinning him round so he was facing the wrong way. The look he gave the boy and his father was vicious. They did it deliberately, he knew it.

He spun the steering wheel, trying to get the car facing the right way, but no luck. He was swamped by cars coming at him: bump! bump! bump! He was imprisoned, trapped, shouted at by other kids. They didn't have a clue what they were doing but he was the one who finally had to be rescued by the attendant, who said to him: 'Try and keep going forward! You're blocking things up, mate!'

Him blocking things up! He was the one trying to show them how it was done!

He finished the ride grimly, keeping as far as possible away from everyone else, especially girls and little Batman. It ended far too soon. He tried to stay in the car but the attendant made him get out and pay again. Altogether he went on five times, always in the same red car, which was a Ferrari, and he was Michael Schumacher.

Dianne recovered enough to go on with him at the

end. She insisted on taking the wheel when she got in and then started deliberately slamming into every car she came across. His head kept getting snapped back and his cheeks were red with shame.

'It's what you're supposed to do, kiddo,' she told him, as they got mixed up in smash after smash and the attendant had to come and rescue them again and again. Dianne was laughing her head off, flirting with the attendant. Her eyes were gleaming and she was tossing back her hair, with only one hand on the wheel.

'That was great,' she said when it was mercifully over and the attendant was helping her out of the car, his hand lingering on hers, Chook noticed.

They were past the exit barrier when Chook took a last look back at his red Ferrari that Dianne had abused so badly. It was empty. All the cars were empty. The fair was closing soon and people were heading for home. The attendant was about to shut the ride down.

'Can I have one last go?' Chook asked suddenly.

Dianne checked her money.

'All right,' she said. 'If Grant will let you. Lucky last.'

Chook ran to buy a ticket and showed it at the gate to the attendant, Grant, who looked reluctant till Dianne smiled at him. Grant winked at her and let Chook through. Chook slid into his Ferrari, belt snapped shut, ready. The music swelled again as Grant started the ride going. Chook was off and racing. It was his dream ride, the best one of all, with nobody to get in his way. It was the one he'd wanted from the beginning. Smooth and sweet. He spun round and round the track, brilliantly avoiding imaginary crashes. The steering wheel responded to his every wish. The car purred beneath him and he had everything to live for, everything was looking rosy. He waved across to Dianne when he passed her but she was laughing up at Grant, who didn't have anything to do but flirt, now he had an expert rider like Chook on the track.

Then the music changed and he realised what song they were playing through the tinny speakers. Kylie. 'I Should Be So Lucky'. He laughed out loud and looked round again at Dianne. She noticed it too and started dancing and singing along, over by the exit barrier. 'I should be so lucky!' He roared out the chorus and gave Dianne the V for victory signal.

He wanted it never to end, just him and the car forever, but Grant finally dragged himself away from Dianne, looked at his watch and flicked off the switch. Kylie went into slow mo and the red Ferrari gradually came to a stop.

CHAPTER FOURTEEN

NO WAY OUT

Chook doesn't know how long he's stayed in the car but it's got so hot, sweat is pouring down his face. When he looks in the rear vision mirror he sees the purple mercurochrome on his cheeks has run and mixed with dirt from where he's wiped his face. He keeps an eye on his dad, who hasn't moved, making cup after cup of bitter black coffee and slowly spreading vegemite on bread.

Chook doesn't feel hungry. His lip still hurts and his cheeks still sting when he rubs at them. He is sticking to his vow not to eat and not to leave the car. His stomach feels tight and hot. He lines all of his cars up along the dashboard in order of importance from left to right. His hands are clammy with sweat and he has trouble picking each one up. The Mustang leads from the Charger and the RX7, then comes the Porsche and the Corvette, with the Camaro and the Hummer last. Then he changes them all round and puts them into two groups, those with spoilers and those without.

The sun is blasting in the front windscreen, its rays bouncing off his cars. He puts his hat on and pulls it down low. As he winds down the window to try to cool off, he sees his dad walking towards him. He feels a twinge of fear in his stomach and moves across into the passenger seat so he's further away. He looks straight ahead.

His dad opens the driver's door.

'Are you going to get out?' he asks.

'Nope. I'm staying here till we move on.'

'You'll have a long wait.'

Chook shrugs.

His dad goes on: 'I heard a couple of cars leaving the camping ground. Thought we might go along and see what's doing.'

Chook shakes his head. His dad makes a move as if he will hit him or haul him out of the car. Chook grabs onto the passenger door handle, just in case. His dad does not realise how desperate it is for them to get out of here.

Kev stops short of hitting him again. He seems to check himself and says: 'I hit you before because with Max and that ... whole business ... I flipped when I saw the bloody makeup.'

Chook says nothing.

His father adds, as if it's a joke: 'Don't want you turning into a fuckin poof.'

Chook shakes his head again and looks at his dad pityingly. How could he think that? If he's a poof, how come he's got a girlfriend? He's no poof. And Max isn't one either. He hasn't got married because he hasn't found the right girl yet, that's all. And now he never will.

'Please, Dad, can we leave? We'll get caught if we go back to the camping ground. I know we will. We nearly got caught last time.'

His dad sits down in the driver's seat, fiddling with the keys that Chook has left in the ignition. He doesn't say anything. Chook sneaks a glance at him. He still looks as if he needs taking care of, but why does he make it so hard for Chook to love him?

After a bit of fiddling, Kev says: 'You know that night, with Max ... I come home with Jimmy about eleven-thirty and I seen his ute still there and something made me suspicious. I'd been a bit suss anyway ever since he bought you that bike. So I come in, I sort of crept in, didn't turn on the light, come straight through into the bedroom. I pulled the covers back. Max had no clothes on, in bed with you. You had none on neither. He had a hard-on.'

Chook says: 'I didn't hear you come home.'

'I lost it completely. Decked him, straight out.'

Chook is silent.

His dad goes on: 'We'll move on soon. I promise. I wanted to keep out of sight … See, I can't decide where to go. I was planning to go to Adelaide and leave you with Les but now … they'll be watching his place.'

'Why, Dad? Has Les done something bad too?'

'No, but they know he's a mate of mine. We were in Boronia together. It's a piss-off because I wanted him to look after you if anything happened … I can't stay long in South Aus myself because I skipped parole there once.'

Chook doesn't see why he can't go back to the farm. He can take care of himself, help Jimmy with the sheep, earn some money. He'll need a job, anyway, if they get his dad. He starts to tell his dad what he wants to do but Kev cuts him off.

'Don't be stupid. They won't let you.'

'Who's "they"?' Chook asks.

'The bloody Welfare. The do-gooders. They'll make you go to school and that. They'll probably put you in bloody foster care, like they done with my sisters. I don't want that to happen to you. But I'm still trying to think who could look after you.'

His dad sounds sort of sad, as if he's given up on every plan. Chook knows where he wants to go.

'Couldn't I go back up north, Dad? Amber's mum and dad might have me.'

His dad says: 'There's no way they'll have you. They hate my guts.'

'But they like me,' Chook says.

His dad reminds him they've already got two children of their own, but Chook says it's worth a try. They both know Chook wouldn't be any trouble because he can look after himself. He can live out on the verandah or in their car, depending if it's big enough. He's not sure what they're driving now. Even he would be too long for some of those girl cars, like Daihatsu Charades.

'I'll have to make a few phone calls when we get somewhere. See what I can set up.'

'That's why I want to get moving, Dad. So we can find a phone. Please?'

His dad is about to answer when they turn towards the sound of a car coming along the bank, then relax, realising it's the rangers. The white vehicle comes into view, Reg driving as usual, with Lyall by his side. There's no sign of Cliff. They pull up next to the Corolla and sit for a moment, keeping their eyes down.

'I wonder what they want,' Kev says. 'Maybe they've found some pituri.'

He gets out and straightens up to speak to them as Chook starts to get out.

'Or maybe they've come to take us on a tour,' Chook calls excitedly to his dad. It will be their own private tour.

Then he hears his father shout.

'Get back in the car! Get in the car!'

Bewildered, he half falls back and sees his dad fling himself into the driver's seat and turn the key. The engine does not want to turn over after the bumpy ride it had getting here, and then sitting idle for two days. It groans and makes a dull whirring sound but finally starts under his father's repeated, urgent pressure on the accelerator. Out his window, Chook can see that two cops have got out of the back of the rangers' four wheel drive and have got their weapons aimed at them.

His father shouts at him: 'Get down!' But Chook has already ducked down in his seat. His dad guns the car into action and floors it along the bumpy bank, dodging tree branches and rocks. Chook has a job staying where he is, doubled up on the front seat. He tries to hang on to anything he can, the door handle, the back of the seat, but keeps losing his grip. His small cars are flung off the dashboard and fly round the car. He feels one hit him on the arm. He hears shots being fired and tries to get even lower. The cops must be trying to kill them.

He hears his father say 'fuck' and feels the car stop momentarily, then turn violently to the right and then to the left again, the wheels spinning, the car bucking and rearing out of control like a runaway stallion. Chook is catapulted off the seat, bruising his already damaged face on the dashboard and ending up on the floor. They career along wildly for a few metres till they slam into a tree, the car lifting up on two wheels as if in a desperate bid to escape gravity, then settling back onto four.

He can hear another vehicle screeching to a halt nearby. Their engine has stopped and a smell of burning comes from under the bonnet. Chook stays where he is on the floor, waiting for the cops to come and finish him off. Then he sees his dad madly locking all the doors and crawling through the gap between the front seats, hauling Chook after him.

'Get in the back. Stay down and get in the back,' his father urges him. The two of them sprawl into the back in a tangle of legs and arms, ending up on top of each other, hearts thudding together.

'What's happened?' Chook pants.

'Fuckin cops everywhere. They've got us surrounded. Reg and Lyall must have given us up. Fuckin dogs.'

Chook wants to cry. It's his doing. But they found them faster than he expected.

'What are we going to do?'

'Nothing we can do. Stay here, that's all.'

An age seems to pass. They can hear vehicles moving round fast, scraping on rocks. Revving out, then stopping. Doors opening and shutting. They lie together on the back seat. His dad must have banged his head on the steering wheel. He has blood running down his forehead, dripping onto Chook. The pause turns into a tense silence.

Then they hear a voice over a megaphone: 'Kevin, this is the police. We've got you surrounded. What we want you to do is to get out of the car slowly with your hands in the air. We know Douglas is there with you and we don't want anyone hurt. There will be no shooting from us if you co-operate. Just get out with your hands in the air and there'll be no trouble.'

The voice stops. Kev and Chook lie still.

'Why don't they come and get us?' Chook whispers. 'What are they waiting for?'

'Maybe they think we've got a gun.'

'We haven't.'

'They don't know that.'

'I've got my Swiss army knife, Dad. We can use that.'

His dad doesn't answer. He looks as if he didn't hear.

'How did they find out my name is Douglas?' Thinking to himself, not that it is.

'Must have looked up your records. Birth certificate.'

They lie still, waiting.

After a while the megaphone comes again: 'You

can't win this one, Kevin. It's best for the boy not to prolong things. Just get out of the car with your hands up and there'll be no dramas.'

Tears start pouring down Chook's face. He hugs his dad even tighter, feeling the beads from his dad's wristband pressing into his arm. He thinks guiltily about the anklet he threw away. Now they'll be split up forever and it's all his fault.

'I won't let them take you away, Dad.'

'They ain't got me yet,' Kev says.

'Why can't we drive away, Dad?'

'They got us blocked in.'

'Where are Reg and Lyall?'

'Who fuckin cares?'

'I love you, Dad.'

'I love you, Chook.'

Kev clutches Chook so tightly it hurts. His chest heaves and he buries his face in Chook's hair. Chook can hardly breathe. He moves slightly to try to get his breath but his dad doesn't seem to notice.

Then they hear the megaphone again: 'You haven't got a choice, Kevin. There's nowhere to go. It's best to give yourself up now.'

Kev holds Chook even tighter, if that is possible.

'Think about Douglas, Kevin. You're making it harder on him, you realise. Please give yourself up. Get out of the car now.'

They stay where they are, Chook feeling his father's full weight on him, the urgency of his heartbeat. There is silence all round them for a while, like the quiet before you get a belting. Chook pictures the cop cars surrounding them in a tight circle, waiting it out with guns drawn, like in the movies. He hopes they'll be able to get out of here without being shot. He is crushed under his father's weight and makes another tiny movement to get more air. Again his dad seems not to notice. They wait hopelessly for whatever will come next.

It is the sound of breaking glass. Chook lifts his head for a moment and sees cops in flak jackets smashing the windscreen and the front windows of the car. He and his dad duck down, away from the flying glass. While they have their heads down, cops storm into the car and sit on top of them, unlocking the back doors and crushing Chook even more. He thinks he's going to suffocate before they shoot him.

Both back doors are pulled open at the same time and more flak-jacketed figures drag Kev and Chook out of the car. In a daze, Chook can hear shouts and cries and running feet scuffing the dirt. He kicks and screams at them to leave him and his dad alone. For a moment he can't see his dad and tries to escape. Two men get hold of him from behind to stop him running away. Then he sees his father lying on the ground nearby with three men kneeling on him to hold him down.

'Leave my dad alone!' he screams.

One of the men holding him says soothingly: 'Don't worry. They won't hurt him.'

Chook sees them handcuff his dad's hands behind his back, then they get him to his feet, ready to march him over to the police car that first blocked their way. Chook sees there are only four vehicles, including the rangers' car, not nearly as many as he imagined. The first cop car must have swung into their path, forcing his dad to spin the wheel sideways so they ended up against the tree. The other cars are parked further back along the bank. There are about a dozen armed cops, four of them with his dad, two with him and the rest already buzzing round Dr Khan's car and their campsite like blowflies round rotten meat.

Kev looks over to where the two men are holding Chook.

'You take good care of him,' he calls out to them.

Chook yells: 'Dad!'

Kev says: 'It'll be OK, mate.'

Chook keeps on calling out to his dad and wriggling and kicking, trying to get away from the men who are holding him, as they walk his dad over to the cop car and put him in the back. Chook sees its number plate is the same as the one parked outside

Maryanne's place. XLY 320. Maryanne's boyfriend must be here. Good thing his dad doesn't realise that. Two cops get in the front, two in the back on either side of Kev, and they take off along the bank.

Chook screams again: 'Don't take him away. I want to go with him!'

The same man who spoke before says: 'They're taking him to Broken Hill. We'll take you there too, don't worry. You'll see him at the station.'

Chook calms down a bit when he hears that. As long as he can see him again. As long as they aren't lying to him.

The two cops now stand Chook up and start walking him over towards another cop car. One of them says as they walk: 'We've had lots of people putting their hands up for you, Doug, after they saw you on the TV news. We had a couple of calls from somewhere up the coast, where was it again, Mac?'

The other cop, Mac, says: 'Nambucca way, I think, Hop.'

'Yep. Somewhere like that. They all want you, Doug. You certainly looked a bit more angelic in the pictures than you do right now, but we'll get you fixed up. There's a big feed and a hot shower waiting for you at a house back in town. Are you hungry?'

Chook doesn't answer. If it's at Maryanne's house, he's not hungry. He'll stay in the cell with his dad and starve.

Mac says: 'You're in good hands now, Doug.'

Chook shouts at him: 'Don't call me Doug!' and tries to twist away from them. 'I've got to get my stuff!'

'We'll get everything, don't worry,' Hop says, holding on to him more tightly.

'Come on, calm down,' Mac says. 'We'll take care of everything.'

'What about my cars!' Chook screams. 'They're in the Corolla.'

The rangers are still standing near their car, parked in its original position. He sees Reg and Lyall go over to the Corolla and look for his cars which he knows are scattered all over the floor. They gather them up, together with his cap, and walk over to the cop car where Chook is being held, his face streaked with purple tears. They hand them to him, keeping their eyes down. Chook can see they are embarrassed. He counts quickly to check the cars are all there.

Reg whispers to him: 'The missus saw you blokes on the TV news last night. We phoned the cops after you left this morning.'

Lyall adds: 'The cops made us show them the way in.'

And Reg says: 'It was your dad beating you up that got to us.'

Chook nods. He puts his cap on his head and with his hands wrapped round the cars, he raises one in a sort of awkward wave to them, as if saying thanks and goodbye.

Reg puts an arm out and touches him on the shoulder. 'Come back here some time soon. We'll take you out bush.'

Chook nods again and, still clutching the cars in both hands, gets into the cop car, another white four wheel drive. One cop gets in the front and the two who've been holding on to Chook all along get in the back either side of him.

'What about the rest of our stuff?' Chook asks.

'They'll bring it. There's another carload of blokes here,' Mac says.

'But the gas and the stove belong to the rangers.'

'They'll sort it out.'

'And Dr Khan's car? Will they bring that?'

'Don't worry. It'll all be taken care of.'

He looks back at Dr Khan's car. It's a mess, with two flat tyres the cops must have shot out and the whole of one side smashed in where it collided with the tree. She is not going to be pleased. He puts his cars back into his pockets where they belong, the Porsche and the RX7 crowding against his Swiss army knife.

They go lurching and rolling along the bank, past the rangers standing forlornly by their car. They both raise their hands in a final wave, then Chook sees them get into their car and begin to follow them out.

Hop asks: 'It was you that rang the Flying Doctors, wasn't it?'

'Maybe,' Chook mutters, unwillingly.

'You done good, kid. The doctor hadn't been found till then.'

Chook doesn't say so, but he's glad. She didn't deserve to be tied up.

'Is she all right?' he has to ask eventually.

'A bit stiff and sore, but she's fine.'

When they get near the camping ground, Chook sees all the campers standing in a knot, straining to see the action, like people at an accident. They are too far away to have seen what happened but they must have been able to hear it. Chook thinks they look like scavengers waiting for road kill. Ron and Val are there, he sees. He recognises them by the blue terry towelling hat Ron still has on. Overfed pigs. He reaches past Mac, puts the window down, and sticks his finger up at them.

'That'll be enough of that!' Mac says. 'It's not their fault.'

'They should have gone on the tour,' Chook says.

Mac looks puzzled but Chook doesn't bother to explain that he's mad at them for caring more about stuffing their fat faces and having soap in the toilets than going to see the engravings and learning about Koori history. They could have looked around them

and seen some really important stuff, instead of lining
their shoes up in neat pairs and complaining about
crap that doesn't matter. Mac puts the window back up
to keep out the dust, as they turn onto the road
leading away from the park. Chook keeps his gaze on
the road ahead, willing the driver to go faster and catch
up with his dad.

He puts his hands into his pockets, feeling for the
Camaro his dad gave him. He knows its shape. When
he finds it, he curls his fingers tightly round it and
makes a wish that Dr Khan will still be able to fly him
back to the farm, now her car's a write-off. After all,
that wasn't his dad's fault, it was the cops. It wouldn't
take her very long. She wouldn't need to stick round
once she'd checked on Max. She could get back on
board and take off, leaving him behind to pick up the
rest of his cars and the gold sovereigns and the money
out the back in the tin, as well as some warm clothes
for his dad that he'll be sure to need in prison. It's
always very cold there because the walls are made of
stone and in the movies they always have water
dripping down them.

Then he'll get on Striker and ride all the way into
Bathurst, past the sheep with their noses pressed against
the windows, past the haunted house, past the park
where the fair comes every year. His heart leaps at the
thought there might be dodgems, but he won't stop for

more than one or two goes before he rides on to the railway station. With the money from the tin, he'll buy a ticket to Macksville for him and Striker and when they get there, he'll make ten calls to Dianne's mobile till he gets the right last number and she'll come and pick him and Striker up and take them to Taylor's Arm. 'Great to see you, kiddo!' she'll say.

Once he gets the plan set in his head, he sits back in his seat and almost relaxes.

Hop looks at him and puts his hand on his head, saying: 'That's better ... We'll take good care of you, mate. No worries.'

Chook moves his head away and doesn't reply. He is still looking straight ahead. They must have gained on the car carrying his dad, because he suddenly sees it round a rare bend in the almost straight, flat road. He strains to try to catch a glimpse of him inside, but a big plume of dust churned out by his dad's car spins back and wraps itself round them, turning their world red.

Mac says: 'Jeez!' And Hop jokes: 'Your dad still kicking dirt in our faces, eh, Doug?'

The cop driving is forced to put his foot on the brake, slowing right down to let the car ahead get away. When Chook can finally see again, his dad has vanished.

ACKNOWLEDGMENTS

I wish to thank all at Varuna, the Writers' House, in Katoomba, who have assisted me at crucial stages in the development of this novel: particularly its director, the wise and wonderful Peter Bishop, and my two mentors, Tegan Bennett and Charlotte Wood, whose contribution has been invaluable. At HarperCollins, my editor, Vanessa Radnidge, has given unstinting support and enthusiasm and the publisher, Linda Funnell, has made excellent structural suggestions. In the latter stages, Kim Swivel's edit much improved the book.

I also thank my agent, Annette Hughes, and many friends and readers, including Victoria Cleal, Robyn Blissett, Anne Marie Droulers, Ros and Andy Doldissen, Anne England, Lyn Lee and Don and Joan MacPherson. In Broken Hill I was greatly assisted by the librarians of the archive there, and by Ralph Wallace, president of the Historical Society, who gave me a special tour of the mosque museum. Thanks to the rangers at Mutawintji National Park for taking me on one of their cultural tours and also to Greg and his family who adopted me off an early morning train on one of my many visits to Broken Hill, warmed me up and showed me around. In

Bowraville, Diane O'Donnell shared her extensive local knowledge with me.

Above all to my family: Paul, Alex, Nina and Madeleine, thanks for everything.

P.S.

Ideas,
insights
& features
included
in a new
section…

Meet Denise Young

Denise Young was born and educated in Sydney, graduating with a first class honours degree in English from the University of Sydney. An academic career beckoned, but she chose to leave the university, working as a high school English teacher both in Sydney and in London, then moving to New Zealand after marrying New Zealand film maker Paul Maunder.

The marriage revived a long-held interest in drama and acting and after attending the National Drama School in New Zealand, Denise worked on various local film and television projects and also in the Amamus theatre group directed by Paul Maunder, which toured collectively written plays to all parts of the country as well as to a theatre festival in Wroclaw Poland, via a season in London.

Denise returned to Australia in 1977 and spent two years in Adelaide studying for a Master of Arts in Drama with Professor Wal Cherry at Flinders University. From there she accepted a job at Curtin University of Technology in Perth teaching theatre. This led to an involvement in the theatre scene in Perth, where she directed a youth theatre team and performed at all major theatres as an actress, including playing Sonya in Anton Chekhov's *Uncle Vanya* opposite the British actor Timothy West, which was a real highlight of her career.

Denise also began to write plays at this time, though she had for years contributed as an actor to group pieces. She set up the Fremantle Theatre Group and co-wrote with two others *Last Tango in Paradise* and *Dirty Tricks in Toy Town*, both performed at the Perth Institute of Film and Theatre.

Back in Sydney in 1986, she taught Theatre Studies at the University of New South Wales until the late nineties, when she decided to leave and try writing prose rather than plays. *The Last Ride* (filmed as *Last Ride*), Denise's first book, is the result of that decision. ∎

Life at a Glance

- Highly commended, Davitt Award for Best Adult Crime Novel by an Australian woman, 2005
- Shortlisted, Fellowship of Australian Writers, Christina Stead Award for Fiction, 2004
- Winner, Fellowship of Australian Writers, Jim Hamilton Award for Best Unpublished Manuscript, 2003
- Winner, HarperCollins Varuna Awards for Manuscript Development, 2002 ∎

Top ten
favourite books

Housekeeping
Marilynne Robinson

Wuthering Heights
Emily Brontë

Youth: A Narrative and Two Other Stories
Joseph Conrad

Anna Karenina
Leo Tolstoy

Madame Bovary
Gustave Flaubert

A Life's Music
Andreï Makine

The Sea
John Banville

That Eye, the Sky
Tim Winton

The Secret River
Kate Grenville

The Blind Assassin,
Margaret Atwood

Varuna, the Writers' House, and the HarperCollins Varuna Awards

by Denise Young

When I first went to Varuna in May 2000 for a one-day workshop led by fellow writer Charlotte Wood, called 'A Leap Into Fiction', I had no idea I was taking the first step on a journey that would see me return again and again to Varuna and would culminate with the publication by HarperCollins of my first novel, *The Last Ride* in May 2004.

The book passed through each of Varuna's professional development programs and came out the other side immensely improved. It was selected for a development forum in 2001 with Tegan Bennett, a follow-on mentorship later that same year, coincidently again with Charlotte Wood, and a Varuna Award for Manuscript Development with HarperCollins in April 2002.

Each time I was surprised that the book continued on its merry way, each time sure that now it had met its match and I, my comeuppance, but on we marched, the book and I, to the heady heights of publication. It richly deserves to be called a Varuna book, though it wears that imprint lightly. Varuna was a careful and helpful midwife, but the book still felt like mine. It is the highest tribute to Varuna to say that the books assisted by them are completely diverse.

Writing a first novel is a step into the unknown: one is assailed by doubts and haunted by insecurities: can I, should I, dare I, will I, how will I? Before that first workshop, I had begun, then turned my back on, many, many stories. I had written plays before and some essays, but a novel seemed beyond me. Even before the first week-long development forum I had virtually abandoned the story and planned to tell Varuna I would not be taking up any offer as I was working on something else now. Of course the minute the phone call came offering me a place I knew there was no way I was missing the chance.

What followed proved to be exactly what I needed; faith, confidence, brainstorming with other writers, connections forged with them, the right questions asked at the right time, and an all-consuming creativity I experienced during two magical stays at Varuna. All of these elements went to make up a supportive program for a very unsure first novelist. Without Varuna's involvement I know I would still be wondering if I could ever write anything.

Varuna is a rare and special place, its director Peter Bishop and the fine writers who work as mentors, rare and special people. In the annals of Australian writing it has already earned its place. Its collaboration with HarperCollins has opened up access to professional editing and publishing opportunities for many new and emerging writers. I will be forever grateful to both Varuna and HarperCollins that, with a safety net beneath me, I leapt into fiction. ■

> ❛ I had begun, then turned my back on, many, many stories ❜

On Set with Hugo, Tom and Mr Right

by Denise Young

It's no limo that delivers me to Quorn in outback South Australia to visit the set of the movie *Last Ride.* I've got butterflies in my stomach and deep misgivings as I putter up in the gutless pram with an engine that I hired in Adelaide, through the flatness of Spencer Gulf country towards Port Augusta: misgivings about what I'm doing there and how I'll be treated. After all, I've seen *Adaptation,* where the writer Charlie Kaufman is evicted from the set of *Being John Malkovich* for getting in the cameraman's eyeline, and Mac Gudgeon, the scriptwriter who turned my book into the movie currently being shot, told me writers were about as much use on set as spare pricks on a honeymoon.

There's a bigger question as well. *The Last Ride* is my baby. Strangers are about to turn my baby into another kind of beast altogether. Will I like or hate what I see?

Everything seems good on paper. Mac showed me the first two drafts of the film script, even though he wasn't obliged to under the terms of the contract, and he encouraged my feedback. I felt that he'd stayed true to the spirit of the book and, above all, that he loved my two main characters, father and son, Kev and Chook, as much as I did. Indeed I thought that as a man he'd found some other more masculine elements in that relationship. However I haven't seen the final shooting script and don't even know how it ends. The endings

> ❝ Will I like or hate what I see? ❞

that Mac has come up with in the drafts I've seen so far are more dramatic than the one I chose in the book, but I'm prepared to trust his vision, knowing that film demands a more dramatic climax than literature.

The director, Glendyn Ivin, and the director of photography, Greg Fraser, are both highly regarded. Producers Nick Cole and Antonia Barnard have steered the film through all the hoops and hoopla with love and terrier-like intensity, snapping at the heels of funding bodies till they got the money to make it.

Nick bought the option to turn my novel into a film six years earlier, before it was published. He'd seen the manuscript courtesy of our shared agent. The option ran initially for three years then was renewed for another three. During that six years Nick moved steadily through the various stages required to get a film funded. First of all he engaged the Melbourne scriptwriter Mac Gudgeon, author of many television scripts and the film *The Delinquents*, and the various drafts of the script were then funded by Film Victoria. Another producer came on board, the very experienced Antonia Barnard, one of whose recent productions was *The Painted Veil*. Then an up-and-coming director, Glendyn Ivin, became attached to the project. Glendyn had won a prize at Cannes for his short film *Cracker Bag* in 2003 and was looking at various ideas for his first feature film. He told me later that what drew him to it was its exploration of the father–son relationship. Finally, internationally and locally acclaimed actor Hugo Weaving committed. Films need all these alignments of enthusiasm from big and well-respected names to ▶

❝ I'm prepared to trust his vision ❞

**On Set with Hugo, Tom and
Mr Right** *(continued)*

attract funding from government and private investors if they're to have a show of attracting even the minimal budgets they need. This film's budget is four million dollars.

I hiccup into Quorn looking for the unimaginatively named Fifth Street. It isn't hard to find. They go in order in the tiny and very attractive town, with broad streets, old stone houses and an ancient steam train that runs on the weekends through the Pichi Richi cut. I see that Fifth Street is blocked off with tape to stop cars entering, and there are the usual large vans and film people bustling purposefully about. There's a crowd of neighbours hovering, waiting for excitement to strike.

Somebody with an armful of costumes is getting out of one of the ubiquitous four-wheel drives that power and transport a film's cast and crew when I pull up, so I nervously introduce myself. Her reaction is reassuring: 'Oh how wonderful to meet you. I loved your book!'

The producers were kind enough to order a dozen copies of my book for cast and crew to read while they were hanging round on set. It's remarkable how many people have read it and come up to talk to me about the book. I'm not silly enough to believe they all loved it, but at least the presence of the book on set gives credibility and respect to the work on which the movie is based.

I spot Hugo Weaving, who is playing the main character, Kev. He comes straight up to tell me that he also loves my book and

> ❛ There's a crowd of neighbours hovering, waiting for excitement to strike ❜

relishes playing the character of Kev, a violent man, but one who in his own way loves his ten-year-old son, Chook, and is trying to do the best he can, according to his not very bright lights. Hugo's passion and commitment to the project shine out and, no matter what the result, I know instantly that there is deep integrity as well as talent at work here.

Tom Russell, the boy playing Chook, is a great choice. He looks wonderful and his acting is instinctive and 'in the moment'. He and Hugo already seem to share an easy rapport, which is important as the impact of the film depends on the relationship between these two, who are almost never off screen. And Tom adores the Jack Russell, Mr Right, introduced into the film as the pet dog of Kev's girlfriend Maryanne. This feels freaky because I had no Jack Russell in my book but have just lost a much-loved one as a pet.

The whole crew seem to share Hugo's passion for the project. I'm told again and again how beautiful this film is going to be. 'Think Wim Wenders with an Australian accent,' they assure me. Even allowing for the hype and enthusiasm that comes from a shared endeavour, this is heady stuff.

There is one slight hitch: they're not actually shooting any scenes from my book while I'm there. All the scenes being shot during my two days on set are new ones from Mac Gudgeon's script. I've missed the dawn shoot where Kev and Chook wake up in a cemetery and steal flowers from graves to take back to former girlfriend Maryanne's house, in the hope that if she's home the flowers will sweeten things between her and Kev. ▶

" Hugo's passion and commitment to the project shine out "

On Set with Hugo, Tom and Mr Right *(continued)*

I arrive in time to see the two forlorn figures, carrying cheap luggage and limp sleeping bags, turn up on Maryanne's front porch and present her with the flowers. The house's real owner, Tim, is ever present on set. In the movie, Maryanne is living with a home renovator and Tim's house was chosen because it was in a partially renovated state. Unfortunately before the shoot started Tim was unable to resist doing a bit more work and the producers have had to beg him to leave the kitchen unrenovated.

Over dinner that night Glendyn shares with me, via his laptop, some stills already shot and some locations coming up. They reveal a dark, moody intensity and a landscape whose vast emptiness mirrors the moral and emotional emptiness within Kev. The landscape looks as if it will truly be a character in the movie, with the inspiring red terrain of the Flinders Ranges a particular highlight. Though I set my book around Broken Hill I can see that the locations the producers and director have chosen are more than its equal.

One new element introduced into the shooting script comes from Glendyn's life, he tells me. It's a memory from his Melbourne childhood of seeing a neighbour killing, skinning and butchering a sheep in his backyard. He has Chook watching from the car window as his father's friend, Max, does just this. This moment of horror mirrors some of the horrors he has already witnessed in his young life. Also, instead of Max coming from yet another Australian farmhouse, as he does in my book, Glendyn

> " The landscape looks as if it will truly be a character in the movie "

has found a perfect post-industrial, semi-rural place for him to live and work in: a car wrecking yard on the edge of town. This fits perfectly with the harsh events that unfold there and gives a quite different visual interest. I like these changes. They create visual metaphors where the book has to rely on words.

Glendyn also tells me of an upcoming scene to be shot on a huge salt lake in South Australia, Lake Gairdner, where father and son quarrel in the car and Kev puts the boy out and drives off. The image of the small boy plodding across the vast dry lake sends shivers up my spine. Again, this is the stuff film can do that no amount of written description can achieve.

The crew of around thirty people (small by international film standards) are currently shooting week two of a six-week schedule. They still have large parts of outback South Australia to traverse, from Woomera to the Flinders and back to Adelaide. It is, Antonia confides later, a very tiring shoot, with such an intense emphasis on two main characters, including a child actor who cannot be worked as hard as an adult and locations throughout the outback that are universally freezing. They wake up to mornings with ice on the windscreens of the cars, and so on. Film shoots must be the most cohesive, collaborative and intense periods, with so many people working away from home at such close quarters. They are the polar opposite of working alone as a writer, when, in the privacy of your study/bedroom/attic/(or coffee shop if you're J.K. Rowling), you create characters which, one day if you're lucky, someone may want to bring to life and animate through ▶

❝ They create visual metaphors where the book has to rely on words ❞

**On Set with Hugo, Tom and
Mr Right** *(continued)*

the skill of the scriptwriter, actors, director,
camera, sound, set building, costume and
make up people. Of course this is fraught
with dangers and difficulties for the reader
as well as the writer, who may not see the
characters in the way they are interpreted on
film.

Indeed that is the question people are
most interested in asking me. How does it
feel to see my baby being interpreted by all
these other people? The answer is that it
feels thrilling. I am fortunate to have an
excellent cast and crew, but I've always
understood that film is another animal
entirely. The baby that was and is my book
has been out in the world for nearly four
years. I no longer feel possessive of it. It has
its own life and that life can't be touched by
the movie, which has its own life and being.
My Kev and Chook may not look exactly
like Hugo and Tom and there is no Mr Right
in my book. But the movie is Glendyn and
Mac and Hugo and Tom and Greg and
Antonia and Nicholas and everybody else's
baby now. I will treasure my two days with
people passionate about their work, and
equally passionate about mine.

The film adaptation of The Last Ride
*premiered at the 2009 Adelaide Film
Festival.* ■

The Web Detective

Varuna, The Writers' House
www.varuna.com.au

Critical response to *The Last Ride*
www.deniseyoung.com.au/reviews.html
www.deniseyoung.com.au/media.html

Broken Hill
www.visitbrokenhill.com.au

The Battle of Broken Hill
www.abc.net.au/gnt/history/
Transcripts/s1051016.htm

The old mosque in Broken Hill
www.about-australia.com/travel-
guides/new-south-wales/outback-new-
south-wales/attractions/museum/
afghan-mosque/

Mutawintji National Park
www.visitnsw.com/Mutawintji_National_
Park_p810.aspx

The Afghan camel men
www.southaustralianhistory.com.au/
afghans.htm

***Last Ride,* the film**
www.lastridemovie.com
www.lastrideblog.blogspot.com